FAIR WEATHER

ALSO BY RICHARD PECK

Don't Look and It Won't Hurt

Dreamland Lake

Through a Brief Darkness

Representing Super Doll

The Ghost Belonged to Me

Are You in the House Alone?

Ghosts I Have Been

Father Figure

Secrets of the Shopping Mall

Close Enough to Touch

The Dreadful Future of Blossom Culp

Remembering the Good Times

Blossom Culp and the Sleep of Death

Princess Ashley

Those Summer Girls I Never Met

Voices After Midnight

Unfinished Portrait of Jessica

Bel-Air Bambi and the Mall Rats

The Last Safe Place on Earth

Lost in Cyberspace

The Great Interactive Dream Machine

Strays Like Us

A Long Way from Chicago

Amanda/Miranda

A Year Down Yonder

FAIR WEATHER

A NOVEL BY
RICHARD PECK

Dial Books  New York

Photo on preceding page: Court of Honor, 1893 World's Columbian
Exposition (by permission of the Chicago Historical Society)

Published by Dial Books
A division of Penguin Putnam Inc.
345 Hudson Street
New York, New York 10014

Designed by Lily Malcom
Text set in Garamond
Printed in the U.S.A. on acid-free paper
1 3 5 7 9 10 8 6 4 2

Library of Congress Cataloging-in-Publication Data
Peck, Richard, date.
Fair weather / Richard Peck.
p. cm.
Summary: In 1893, thirteen-year-old Rosie and members of
her family travel from their Illinois farm to Chicago to visit
Aunt Euterpe and attend the World's Columbian Exposition,
which, along with an encounter with Buffalo Bill and Lillian
Russell, turns out to be a life-changing experience for everyone.
ISBN 0-8037-2516-7
1. World's Columbian Exposition (1893: Chicago, Ill.)—Juvenile
fiction. [1. World's Columbian Exposition (1893: Chicago, Ill.)—
Fiction. 2. Chicago (Ill.)—Fiction. 3. Family life—Fiction.
4. Buffalo Bill, 1846–1917—Fiction. 5. Russell, Lillian,
1861–1922—Fiction. 6. Humorous stories.] I. Title.
PZ7.P338 Fai 2001
[Fic]—dc21 00-055561

To Jean and Will Hobbs,
in love and admiration

CONTENTS

1

An Invitation From Aunt Euterpe

10

The Curve of the Earth

25

Christmas in July

40

Faster Than a Galloping Horse

49

Flying to the Moon

59

Bright Lights and Bad Women

72

The Worst Day in Aunt Euterpe's Life
Part One

85

The Worst Day in Aunt Euterpe's Life
Part Two

98
The Greatest Day in Granddad's Life
Part One

110
The Greatest Day in Granddad's Life
Part Two

122
An Invitation for Aunt Euterpe

133
After the Ball

———

135
After the Fair
A Note from the Author

FAIR WEATHER

An Invitation
From Aunt Euterpe

⟡

I t was the last day of our old lives, and we didn't even
know it.

I didn't. It looked like any old day to me, a sultry summer morning hot enough to ruffle the roofline. But then,
any little thing could come as a surprise to us. We were
just plain country people. I suppose we were poor, but we
didn't know it. Poor but proud. There wasn't a blister of
paint on the house, but there were no hogs under the
porch.

I was sitting out in the old rope swing at the back of
our place because the house was too full of Mama and
my sister, Lottie. I wasn't swinging. I thought I was pretty

nearly too old to swing. In the fall I'd be fourteen, with only one more year of school to go.

I was barefoot, bare almost up to the knee. And I wasn't sitting there empty-handed. We were farmers. We were never empty-handed. I was snapping beans in the colander.

After I'd gathered the eggs and skimmed the milk, I'd been out in the timber with a pail for raspberries, wild strawberries, anything going. I'd kept an eye out for mulberries the raccoons might have missed. They loved mulberries. I'd worked up a sweat in the cool of the morning. Now I was enjoying a little quiet here in the heat of the day.

It was all too peaceful to last.

My brother, Buster, was creeping up behind me. He meant to scare me out of my swing and send my beans flying. I snapped on like I was alone in the world. But I knew when he was lurking behind the privy. I knew when he made a dash for the smokehouse. Now I could hear him come stealing up behind me.

Twigs broke. Birds flew off. You'd have to be a corpse not to know. But a boy will pull the same fool stunt over and over like he's just thought of it. He'd be carrying a dead squirrel.

By and by I felt boy-breath on the back of my neck. My hair was in braids. On the nape of my neck I felt a tickle. It might have been a woolly caterpillar off the tree.

But it wasn't. It was the tip end of a squirrel tail. It itched powerfully, but I didn't let on.

He kept it up as a boy will. Presently something hot and clingy dropped over my shoulder. I looked aside and I was eye-to-eye with a dead squirrel, draped there with his little paws dangling down.

As if I hadn't seen every kind of dead animal there is. Many's the time I'd watched Dad gut a pig.

I brushed the squirrel off into the weeds and went on with my work. Buster darted forward, showing himself, and grabbed the squirrel by the tail.

He wore bib overalls and not a stitch else. Fumbling in his pocket, he drew out a folding knife. He had to hold the squirrel by the tail in his teeth to get the blade open.

Squinting, he gripped the squirrel upside down by its hindquarters and made a cut with the knife just above the tail. Then he dropped the squirrel on the ground and tramped his bare foot on the bushy tail to keep it in place. He stooped over, working his fingers into the slit he'd made. Then he stood up right quick, lifting the skin off that squirrel in a single move. A squirrel skins easy. The carcass, pinky-white like a chicken thigh, fell back in the tall grass. Buster held up the pelt, all in one piece like a doll's winter coat.

He was testing me.

Skinning an animal never had fazed me. Neither had killing a snake or shooting a rat in the rain barrel. But I

❀ 4 ❀

was getting on for fourteen now. Buster wondered if I was getting like our older sister. Was I about to start twitching my skirts and telling him how dirty his ears were? Was I going to get skittish and ladylike?

Lottie herself could wring a chicken's neck off with her left hand while whistling "Dixie." And nobody had yet called her dainty. But I knew what Buster was thinking. I always knew. He wondered if I was fixing to grow up and leave him behind.

He flung the squirrel pelt away. There was no use for it. He killed squirrels for the tails. He sold them a penny apiece to the Mepps Lure Company to make spinning lures for fishermen. We'd eat the squirrel, of course— have it with the beans.

Now Buster was digging around in another pocket of his overalls. What next?

He opened his hand, and there sat two hollyhock blossoms—one pink, one lavender—bruised from riding in his pocket. And two hard little hollyhock buds. We had a stand of hollyhocks over by the blackberry briar.

I used to make hollyhock dolls. You needed a full blossom with the petals for the skirt. For the doll's head you fitted a peeled bud where the stem had been. There you had your hollyhock doll. I'd make them in all colors. Lottie showed me how.

Without offering them up, Buster let me see the flowers. But I just shook my head and kept snapping my beans and throwing the stems. I'd grown past hollyhock dolls, and he just as well know. Buster let the breeze take them, as if they didn't matter particularly.

He liked to think he was a quiet man like Dad. But there was too much of Granddad in him. He was never quiet for long. "Shift over, Rosie."

"It's too hot for two in the swing," I said. "Sit on the ground."

"They's chiggers."

So he squeezed in next to me. He wanted to swing, but I planted my feet. "You ought to be out in the field with Dad," I told him. "You're seven, pretty nearly eight."

Dad and the neighbors were in the field that day. I thought Buster ought to be helping, coming along behind to shock up the wheat. He carried water out to them, but rarely lingered. That was my brother all over. Never around unless you didn't want him. He was quicksilver, there and gone again before you knew. Dad himself said he'd never make a farmer out of Buster.

He sat there against me, close as a corn plaster. He'd cut the tail free of the squirrel and was fiddling with it. We sat listening to Mama and Lottie up at the house. You couldn't hear words, but they were getting into the upper register.

Lottie was seventeen that summer, pushing eighteen. She'd gone to all the school she ever meant to. And something had come over her here lately. One of the hired men working for our neighbors the Shattucks was calling on Lottie, and Mama didn't like the turn things might be taking.

They'd been over it many a time. How often had I heard Mama say, "He's a drifter and probably a grifter. We don't know a thing about him. He's not from here. And he's nothing but itinerant labor."

Lottie could fire right back at her, and they'd gone at it hammer and tongs since the late spring when Everett turned up in the district to work for the Shattucks. Though none of this grown-up business was suitable for Buster's ears.

"Do you reckon she'll marry him?" Buster asked. "She'd have to run off."

"Little pitchers have big ears," I said. I didn't want Lottie to haul off and get married any more than Buster wanted me to grow up. But I made the impatient sound sisters make in their throats.

I didn't know if Lottie was thinking of marrying Everett or not. She wasn't talking to me about it.

"If he asked her, she could say no," Buster mused. "It's a free country."

"She doesn't have anything else to do," I said, "but help Mama."

"She could hold off for somebody else."

"Who?" I said. "We live five miles out."

"Maybe he don't want to marry her a'tall," Buster offered.

"And that's another worry," I muttered under my breath.

I didn't suppose anybody would want to marry me when the time came. I had year-round freckles, and my red hair corkscrewed if it was raining in the next county. And I could be a little bit spunky if I had occasion to. I didn't know if men would like that.

But then Buster and I forgot all about Lottie when we saw a dot in the distance. It was coming up the road from the Bulldog Crossing with dust boiling behind. We got very little traffic even in dry weather.

It'd be Granddad Fuller coming back from town in his terrible old wreck of a buggy. Mama wouldn't ride in it. On the slab seat beside him would be Granddad's dog, Tip, who was mostly German police. When they came up to the wind pump, you could hear the clop of hooves. Granddad had his own horse he wouldn't let Dad use. She was a little old gray mare where she wasn't bald. I thought she and Tip were both the same age as Granddad in animal years. The mare was named Lillian Russell.

Granddad went into town every day but Sunday unless we were snowed in. He did our trading for us, and he went for the mail since we didn't have Rural Free Delivery in those days. We no more dreamed they'd bring mail to the house than they'd string electricity out this far. But then we had Granddad.

We didn't get two letters a year, and no bills because we paid cash or bartered. But that didn't keep Granddad at home. He was in town every morning when the post-master opened up.

He took our butter and eggs to sell. If we didn't have mail, Granddad brought the neighbors theirs. If anybody in the district wanted something from the store, he'd bring that. Or if somebody got something they'd ordered out of the Monkey Ward catalog, out that would come. Or he'd carry a message for whoever didn't want to spend a stamp. He came in very handy, and he was the biggest nuisance in the county.

Now he was coming up by the garden at a spanking pace. The spoked buggy wheels flickered past the woven-wire fence. A whip rode in the whip socket, but I never saw Granddad take it out. He used a snaffle in Lillian Russell's mouth because it didn't hurt her like a hard bit. He cared more for that horse and that dog than he cared for the rest of us, as Mama often remarked.

Sometimes he took notice of us. More often his mind was way off in olden times or on other people's business. Today he saw us because he sat up as straight as he could. In the band of his floppy straw hat was a buzzard's feather to ward off rheumatism and the epizootic. Tip looked around him at us.

"Your maw's got a letter!" Granddad hollered out. You could hear that cracked old voice all the way back to town. "It's from Euterpe!"

Buster and I sat on in the swing, taking in this news.

Euterpe, Aunt Euterpe, was Granddad's other daughter. She lived in Chicago.

We couldn't imagine such a place, though there was a steel engraving of the Great Chicago Fire of 1871 hanging in the schoolhouse. Aunt Euterpe never came for a visit, and she didn't write from one year to the next. She rarely came up in Mama's conversation. Somehow I had the notion that Aunt Euterpe had married an old man and vanished from view. She'd never brought her husband home to meet us, and we'd heard tell he was dead.

Buster slid out of the swing and wandered off, like he did. He could just ooze away like a barn cat and not be there. Aunt Euterpe's letter was for Mama, and we'd hear about it when Mama was ready to tell us. Pestering her about anything never worked.

Besides, it might not be good news.

THE CURVE OF THE EARTH

T hough Dad came late from the field, we had our supper in broad daylight. I still see the sunset slanting through the corn rows and across the kitchen table where we sat.

We pulled back, replete with all the squirrels Buster had bagged—squirrels and beans, buttermilk biscuits and a blackberry cobbler. Dad had washed his upper half and put on a clean shirt after his labors. His cheekbones were fire red from the sun, below a forehead white where his hat had been. Granddad hadn't worked up enough of a sweat to change his shirt.

We scarcely spoke while we were at our meal. Aunt

Euterpe's letter, propped against the vinegar cruet, was a silent presence. Now Granddad was drawing out his flick-knife, so Mama said, "Papa, you either mean to pick your teeth with that knife blade or you're going to pare your fingernails. But not at my table."

Granddad looked suspiciously around like we were all in cahoots against him. "When we was settlin' this part of the country," he said in his high croak, "all we had to eat with was a pocketknife for cutlery and a tin plate. That's all we had, and we were happy to have it. I don't recollect when I saw my first fork in this district." His gaze swept us, skipping over Mama.

Buster sat next to me, and something in the side pocket of his overalls jumped. I didn't think much about it. There was at all times something living or dead in Buster's pocket. Lottie sat across from me next to Granddad. The sun was behind her, so I couldn't read her face. But we were all curious about the letter from Aunt Euterpe.

Granddad said, "Ida Postlewaite got a letter from her son today. I brung it out to her." He let a short pause linger, now that he'd brought up the subject of letters. But Mama seemed deaf to him, though her hands worked the napkin in her lap. "That's the Postlewaite boy who lives down by Cahokia," Granddad said, soldiering on, "the one who got that girl—"

"All right," Mama said. "We know who you mean."

Dad stifled a smile.

Another long moment took place. We never lingered idle around the supper table. But there we all sat, growing roots.

Mama folded her napkin, lining up every crease in it till you wanted to scream. She reached into her apron pocket and drew forth her spectacles.

She wore them only for reading, and they gave great purpose to her face. She had a streak of white in her hair that she said Granddad and we children had put there. We thought she was old as the hills. She'd have been thirty-eight that summer. Dad was forty. Granddad was whatever age he wanted you to think he was.

"I suppose you won't be good for anything until you've heard Euterpe's letter," Mama observed.

Wisely, no one spoke.

I sat across the corner of the table from her, watching her unfold the letter. She was holding back, putting off the reading, so now I was wild to know. Mama began, angling the page to catch the light.

My dear sister,
I trust this finds you as it leaves me, tolerably well in the circumstances. We have had a hard winter with the wind straight off the lake and several big boats broken up on ice floes. . . .

I wondered at a woman writing in deep summertime who had to go back to winter for bad news.

*But we have put that behind us. Now the city has
thrown every effort into our fair, the World's
Columbian Exposition, to honor the four-hundredth
anniversary of the discovery of America.*

*I don't know if word has reached you in the country-
side, but the fair is judged the wonder of the age.
President Cleveland was in attendance on the first day.
Spanish nobility has honored us with their presence,
and Paderewski has performed on a Steinway piano.
There is electrical lighting wherever you look.*

Buster sat stock-still, listening. Only his overalls jumped.
Mama read on:

*It is high time the world take notice of this part of
the country. As they say here, Chicago is a cow fed in
Illinois and milked in New York. But the Easterners
have had to sit up and take notice of all that we have
accomplished.*

*Sister, I write to invite you and your children for a
week to see the fair. You no doubt do your best by them,
but they will have seen nothing of the world. Their
vision is limited to the four walls of a one-room country schoolhouse.*

Mama paused and cast her eyes up. We went to the same
one-room schoolhouse that Mama and Aunt Euterpe
had once gone to. Mama continued:

*While there is much at the fair and outside its gates
that is not fit for a child's eyes, I do not know when
your brood will ever have such an opportunity if I do
not provide it.*

*The prices beat anything you ever saw. But you will
be spared the expense of a hotel or a rooming house by
staying with me. The girls can share a bed as they no
doubt do at home. We will find someplace to put the
boy if you see fit to bring him.*

*Entrance to the fairgrounds is fifty cents a head, but
this keeps out the riffraff. I will stand you the price of
admission, and we will go as often as possible, for there
is a good deal to see. I expect no thanks for this.*

*Enclosed in this envelope you will find your tickets
for the Illinois Central Railroad in the chair car.
Though I am not clear in my mind as to your children's
ages, I trust they are all still riding half-fare. I take it
for granted that your husband is too busy to get away
at this time of year.*

The letter began to wind down. Mama was coming to
the foot of the second page. Still Aunt Euterpe hadn't
made mention of Granddad. But then here it came:

*Of course, Papa is out of the question. I expect that
at his time of life, he would sooner keep to his own
fireside.*

As Aunt Euterpe surely knew, we didn't have a fireside.
We had a cast-iron stove to heat the front room. We took
it down in the summer.

A strangled sound rose out of Granddad. He had wat-
tles like a turkey. His Adam's apple wobbled all over his
neck.

Aunt Euterpe concluded:

*Unless I hear word to the contrary, I will meet your
train at the station here on the designated day and
hour. You will know me from afar, as I am still in a
widow's weeds, Mr. Fleischacker having passed over
just four years ago in the spring.*
As ever, your sister,
Euterpe Fuller Fleischacker.

I was dizzy enough by then to pitch off the chair. Just because they were having a world's fair in Chicago didn't
have anything to do with us. I didn't dream we'd go. But
my head spun like a top.

I could feel the vibrations coming off Buster. He was
young enough to think anything can happen. In his head
he already had his traps packed and was off down the
road to flag the train at the Bulldog Crossing.

But not a peep from anybody around the table. Mama
drew four tickets from the envelope and fanned them
out.

Lottie pulled back and put her hands in her lap. We'd never been on a train. We'd been only as far as a horse could pull our Studebaker wagon. We'd been to Decatur once and got lost, and we'd been to Taylorville. We'd been to the Mt. Auburn Picnic. That was about the size of it. To hear him tell it, Granddad had been everywhere. But Aunt Euterpe hadn't invited him to Chicago. I thought he'd say he'd already been up there and didn't like it. But he was silent as the grave.

Mama spoke down the table to Dad. "Gideon, what have you to say about all this?"

Dad's fist had been over his mouth, concealing a toothpick. He shook his head, speechless.

Mama sighed and folded up her spectacles. She was still looking past the cruet at Dad. "Are you easy in your mind about sending your wife and children to a place with a million or so people, most of them criminals, where we're very likely to be robbed on the platform and murdered in the street?"

Dad pondered.

"Well, you would be much missed," he said. There were crinkles around his eyes. He was very dry in his humor, and this wasn't the time for it.

I knew not to blurt out "Can we go, Mama?" And I kicked Buster to keep him still. Across from me Lottie looked too deep in thought to speak. Then she thought of something.

"Aunt Euterpe sounds a hundred years old."

"She's five years older than I am," Mama said. "She'll be forty-four if she lives through the next hard Chicago winter."

"She was born old," Granddad croaked out. "And she married an old geezer because nobody else would have her." Granddad's feelings were hurt, and he was on his high horse. "She had to travel up to Chicago to find him, where they ain't so particular."

"Now, Papa." Mama could be strict, and she was often at the end of her rope. But she had a kind heart.

Hurt though he was, Granddad couldn't keep from sharing with us all he'd heard about the great Columbian Exposition at Chicago. "They've got a big wheel up there you can ride," he said, recovering. "You set in coaches big as Pullman cars. Up you go."

"How high?"

"Oh, I don't know," Granddad said. "Hundreds of feet up."

Buster's eyes were saucers.

Mama didn't mean to listen, and she was all ears. "Do you have to?"

"Have to?" Granddad blinked. "They likely charge you another fifty cents to go on the thing."

"Ah well," Mama murmured, "that's all right then."

"Of course, you can go higher than that," Granddad said. "They've got a captive balloon on the fairgrounds.

That thing will take you so high, you can see the curve of the earth."

Smiling inside, Dad said to Granddad, "That high?"

"Oh, yeah." With a sweep of his hand Granddad showed the curve of the earth.

"I don't know what to do," Mama said quietly, "and I don't have anybody to advise me." She looked around at us, at Buster and Lottie and me. She was thinking we were in dire need of all the education we could get. But there was fear in her eyes, fear of the far-off.

Then she seemed to settle the matter. "I'd as soon not be beholden to Euterpe," she said. "I can't have her laying out that kind of money for us."

"Then you better stuff the tickets in an envelope and send them back," Dad said. "Granddad here can take them in to the post office." The tickets were still in Mama's hands, and Dad was watching her.

All of a sudden Lottie leapt up. Her chair teetered behind her. "Oh, for pity's sake," she burst out, "it's Wednesday night!"

So it was. And the table littered with dishes we hadn't thought to wash up, and pans in the sink. It was Wednesday, and that was the night Lottie let Everett call on her. Regular, like clockwork.

It was time to bustle, and I was ready to clear the table. But I happened to glance at Mama. She was still at her place with the train tickets in her hand. And she was looking up intent at Lottie, studying her. I wondered all evening at that look on Mama's face.

It was gray twilight by the time we'd rung out the dishrags. Lottie dragged two kitchen chairs out to the side porch for her and Everett. I'd noticed she hadn't come to the point of sitting with him in the porch swing.

Granddad went to bed with the chickens. Dad was down at the barn. Buster had made himself scarce, so it was just the three of us in the kitchen, stumbling around a little because it wasn't worth it to light a lamp.

Out of a clear blue sky Mama turned on Lottie. "Go up and put your shoes on before he gets here."

You could have knocked me over with a feather. It was summertime. We didn't put on shoes till Sunday.

"Mama," Lottie said, "he don't see anything but my feet, and he's already seen them."

"Doesn't," Mama snapped. "Not *don't.*"

Lottie bridled. She didn't like being ordered around, then or later. Or corrected.

"I don't give two hoots for this Everett What's-his-name," Mama said, still snappish. "He's here today and gone tomorrow, and I hope he will be. But you can put your shoes on for company, whoever it is. This is 1893, missy, and we're not living in a log cabin."

My land, I thought. But then, Aunt Euterpe's letter

had put Mama in a mood. I skinned out to the porch before she started in on me.

Presently from out there I heard the Sunday sound of Lottie stamping down the stairs in her shoes. Then she stalked onto the porch. It was my habit to sit with her until Everett got there. We sat in the swing with the kitchen chairs looming up beside us.

Once in a great while Lottie and I burst into song out there on the porch, just to pass the time. In those days I sang soprano, and Lottie sang alto. Her voice held mine in the palm of its hand. We only sang the old songs. Where would we hear new ones? We'd sing "Silver Threads Among the Gold" and "Just Before the Battle, Mother," old standbys like those.

There was no music in Lottie's soul this evening. She simmered in silence, still raw over Mama ordering her into shoes. My mind was miles away anyhow. I calculated that Chicago lay in the direction of the smokehouse. I thought if I could just look over the curve of the earth, there Chicago would be. I knew it was on a lake so big, you couldn't see across it. And of course, they were having the fair. I wondered if you'd be blinded for life if there were electric lights wherever you looked.

A small sound from under the porch interrupted my thoughts, a skidding sound over dry leaves. It might have been a snake uncoiling for a night's hunt. But it wasn't.

In a loud voice I said to Lottie, "What do you make of Aunt Euterpe's invitation?"

"It'll blow over," she said. "Mama won't do it."

I elbowed her hard. "You never know, we might go," I said, loud as before. "But Aunt Euterpe don't—doesn't want Buster. You could read that right there in her letter. We'll have to leave Buster behind."

A thump sounded right under our feet. It was very like a head cracking the underside of the floor. I expect Buster reared up right quick in surprise, forgetting he was hiding under the porch to spy on us—and on Everett later. Lottie stamped her heel hard, right about where Buster's head was holding up the porch floor. We heard nothing more but a skittering sound, which might have been field mice, but wasn't.

Then up the road came Everett in a borrowed wagon. He was no hand with a horse, which seemed odd to us. It was a good thing the horse knew more than he did, or they'd be in the ditch.

As he came up by the wind pump, Lottie nudged me out of the swing, and I made myself scarce.

Later on when Lottie and I were ready to turn in, we lit a lamp. As a rule we undressed in the dark. Tonight, though, we thought we'd better not. We slept in a big old spool bed, angled in the room to catch any breeze that blew. In the glare of the lamp Lottie eased her pillow off and examined under it. I did the same on my side. We shook out the pillowcases. Taking her time, Lottie folded the sheet down over the quilt. So did I. Slow and easy Lottie slid back the sheet, and I was just as watchful.

Halfway down the bed a big old bullfrog sprang out. It was a sickly pale green, and its hind legs looked a yard long. Lottie shied as it skimmed her shoulder on the way to freedom. We both shied, though we'd known something was sure to be in the bed. If it was in Buster's pocket at suppertime, it was bound to be in our bed before we were.

With our backs to each other we undressed and pulled on our nightdresses. Lottie kicked her shoes into a corner.

The lamp didn't make the room any cooler, but it was on her side, and Lottie didn't turn it down. She sat propped up in bed with her cheek in her hand. It didn't matter to me. I couldn't see how I'd sleep a wink, with Aunt Euterpe's letter going around and around in my head.

Lottie was going to have Mama's figure, so she took up her full share of the bed. They both had fine big figures. I felt like the runt of the litter.

"Did Everett give you a squeeze?" I inquired.

"At your age," Lottie replied, "I didn't have such thoughts."

"You didn't have a big sister fixing to marry a drifter and a grifter."

"Is that what I'm fixing to do?" Her chin was firm.

"You tell me."

But she didn't, so I said, "Mama thinks so. Mama's worried you'll run off with him."

Lottie shrugged. "Mama's getting crankier than the handle on a churn."

"Aunt Euterpe's letter stirred her up."

"She's not the only one stirred up." Lottie eyed me over her shoulder. Her eyes were violet in the lamplight. Mine were hazel all the time.

"Listen to me, Rosie. You better dismiss Chicago and the fair from your mind. I'll tell you right now: Mama's not going."

"Why not?" I said, trying not to whine.

Lottie sighed. "I suppose it's too late for her. Mama's too old. She wouldn't know where she was up in Chicago. You saw it yourself. She's scared."

"You marrying Everett would scare her worse," I said.

But then I had one of my brainstorms. It was a bolt from the blue, and it liked to knock me out of the bed. "Lottie, did you see how Mama was looking funny at you tonight, after she'd read out the letter?"

"She's been looking funny at me for weeks."

"No, it was different tonight. Lottie, I think we're going to the fair. I think Mama wants to get you away from Everett. I watched her come to that conclusion. Besides, you've seen nothing of the world."

Lottie's eyes grew huge. "And I suppose *you* have?"

"I didn't say so," I answered in a puny voice.

I'd given Lottie food for thought. She sat in the bed,

stroking her cheek, looking down at her bare feet. She had right good-sized feet. They gave her grief later when skirts were shorter.

"Wouldn't you like to see the fair?" I said at last, still in a puny voice.

"It'd be a change, I guess. But they say it's educational, and I don't like the sound of that. I've had enough schooling."

I didn't much like the sound of Aunt Euterpe. "Why do you reckon she's invited us anyhow, Lottie? She's never said boo to us up till now."

"They haven't had a fair up till now," Lottie said, weary.

"What do you reckon Chicago's like?" I said. "It burned down once, you know, but they built it back. And the fair wouldn't be in tents, would it? It'd be grander than that."

But Lottie'd had about enough of me for one night. She was reaching for the lamp. "Rosie, I'll tell you one more time. Mama's dead set against going, so don't build your hopes."

Then in the dark she added, "Besides, what would we wear?"

CHRISTMAS IN JULY

As usual Lottie and I were up and running a little before five the next morning. The scent of coffee rose from the kitchen. Mama was breading pork cutlets for breakfast.

We scanned the table to see if the train tickets were still there. Or if she had put them in an envelope to send back. We saw nothing. Of course, the envelope could be in Mama's apron pocket.

Dad and Granddad had already brought the milk up from the barn. Granddad helped with the milking, since he was up at that hour anyway. But then he figured he'd done his day's chores. Today would be different, as he was soon to learn.

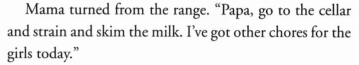

Mama turned from the range. "Papa, go to the cellar and strain and skim the milk. I've got other chores for the girls today."

You should have seen his face. Woman's work! He had a full moustache, white on top and yellow above his lip from his chaw. That moustache nearly twitched off his face. He started to answer, thought better of it, and tramped down the cellar steps.

We did a modest business in butter and eggs, and most of it was left to Lottie and me. There was a good bit of work to it. Butter-making's a two-day process. Since we made butter every day, we were never caught up. You strain the milk, warm from the cow, into pans in the cool of the cellar. Then you skim off the cream and bring it up to the kitchen to ripen for churning. You have to stir at it off and on through the day.

In the afternoons Lottie or I would pour the ripened cream into the churn and churn it by hand. After the butter came, we'd take it out and pour off the buttermilk. Then we'd work the butter with salt and set it in the cellar. The next day we'd bring it up, work it with more salt, and put it into molds.

But something had come over Mama today. She was making changes. And she was not a great one for change.

"Take the big pail for eggs," she told me. "Lift every hen." That meant she wanted extra eggs. I always gathered every one I found, but maybe some days I didn't look as hard as I might.

The egg broker would come to you, but Mama sent butter and eggs into town with Granddad every other day or so. He sold them to the Oldweilers, who ran the store. They put them on the trains to St. Louis and Chicago for the hotels and the eating places there. City people had never tasted a fresh egg in their lives and didn't even know it.

When I came back, dragging a bucket brimming with eggs, the kitchen was hot as hinges even this early in the day.

Lottie was at the drain board, slapping yesterday's butter into molds. Mama banged a platter of fried cutlets into the oven to keep them hot. Then she turned to me. "Hurry on and give me some eggs," she said, as if I wasn't right there by her elbow. Mama was very short with us today, very abrupt in her movements. She was cracking eggs on the edge of the skillet like she was killing vermin.

As I was setting the table, Buster showed up. He sensed trouble and was willing to forgo breakfast in the circumstances. Mama spied him with the eyes in the back of her head as he was reaching for his air rifle.

She wheeled around from the skillet. "There'll be no squirrel hunt today," she told him. "A penny apiece for the tails! That won't pay for the shot."

Buster looked crestfallen.

"I want you and Rosie in the briar as quick as breakfast's over," Mama said. "I want every blackberry you find."

Buster and I swapped glances. I liked roaming the timber, seeing what berries I could find. Picking blackberries in our *briar,* though, was too much like work.

Granddad rose out of the floor with two buckets of cream to ripen. "How does that cream smell?" Mama demanded to know.

Again Granddad looked injured. One time the cows had walked through the fence and got into the mushmelon patch. They ate their fill, and for days afterward the cream smelled like mushmelons. We had to slop it to the hogs. But it only happened once.

"It smells like cream," Granddad growled. "Somebody got up on the wrong side of the bed this morning." He meant Mama, though he was never a ray of sunshine himself before breakfast.

When Dad came in, he'd already done a day's work and was wet through. As we lit into our meal, I saw him glance up the table to see if the train tickets were there. I caught his eye and shook my head, and got away with it.

We finished off in the usual way, with pie—sour cream apple. At the time I supposed everybody in the nation topped off their breakfasts with a big slab of pie. I wondered if we were going to bake today, since we'd be awash in eggs and blackberries.

We were all poised for flight when Mama said in a high, hollow voice, "Papa, I want you to take us to town today."

We all blinked, and Granddad stared. He wore wire-rimmed spectacles down his nose and looked over them, not through them. He was not a great reader.

"Take who?" he said.

"These children," Mama said, ". . . and me."

"Can't be did." He clamped his jaw. "You'd be too big a bunch for the buggy. And I won't leave Tip behind, or he'll pine and get off his feed."

Fat chance of Tip missing a meal is what Mama was thinking. But she said, "There'll be room for us all and Tip too, and the butter and eggs." She glanced at Buster and me. "And the blackberries."

"You tell me how," Granddad muttered.

"Hitch Lillian up to the wagon."

Wherever we went, we hitched one or both of Dad's draft horses to the Studebaker wagon. They were a pair of big chestnut Belgians with white manes. For some reason they were called Fancy Pants and Comet. Of course we couldn't use them today. They'd be with Dad in the field.

"Nosir!" Granddad's fist hit the table. "Draggin' that monstrous big wagon with you and them overgrown kids would put a strain on her. She'd keel over. I won't have it!"

"We won't need to hurry," Mama replied, very calm now. "You run Lillian too hard, Papa. You break her into a gallop on the straightaway. We won't do that today."

Granddad's breath was coming fast. "I don't go to town this early," he said. "The post office don't open till—"

"We'll go at your usual time," said Mama, cool and firm.

"I ain't stayin' all day," Granddad declared. "I ain't got the time for that."

"Neither do we," said Mama. They argued on, and Mama won.

Picking up and going off to town on the spur of the moment was as big a bolt from the beyond as Aunt Euterpe's letter. We went to a country school and a country church. About the only things farmers went to town for in those days were salt, sugar, flour, and baking powder. And we had Granddad.

Being young, we kids liked going to town, but Mama didn't care about it. She was shy among strangers. I didn't know what to think. And before I knew it, I was out in the briar with Buster, fighting the stickers to get to the blackberries.

We went to town that day. But it was a rush and a struggle to get ready. I had to scrub the chicken manure off the eggs before I could pack them in straw, never my favorite chore. Lottie got the cleaner task of scalding the milk pans and setting them outside. Buster had to box up the berries and winnow out all the leaves and twigs, which he didn't like doing.

Out in the lot the air was blue around Granddad as he backed Lillian Russell into the wagon shafts. She kept looking around at him like he'd lost his mind. I gave the cream a quick stir, and we were off down the road to town, our minds swept clean by the novelty of it all.

I picture us yet, rolling along on the crown of the road with all the world we knew fanned out around us. Tip sat on the seat beside Granddad. Mama and Lottie and I rode standing up in the wagon bed, holding on to the sides and each other. We had on fresh aprons to say we were going to town. Mama's had pockets in it. She didn't carry a reticule or a pocketbook. I don't think she owned one. We all wore sunbonnets, the starchy ones we wore away from home, with the strings ironed. We all had on our shoes, except Buster. He rode with his bare feet dangling off the tailgate and his head in the clouds.

Oh, that glorious morning, and we away from our work. When we came to the level Bulldog Crossing with a shanty for a depot, the telegraph wire hummed over us. It was sending its messages we knew not where.

The farms of our neighbors nestled in walnut groves like islands in a sea of grain. The men were in the fields, cutting wheat and oats and barley. They'd wave as we passed, and Mama would nod. Granddad stared straight ahead, mortified on Lillian's behalf. Beside him Tip grinned at the universe. Tip didn't mind how he got there, as long as he got to go.

The men looked up when we passed the Shattuck place, where Everett worked as a hand. Whether he was one who waved, I couldn't see. Whether Lottie took particular notice, I couldn't tell. You could hide much in the depths of a sunbonnet.

As we came up on the town, the houses stood one after another, which made Mama feel crowded. When we stopped in front of the grocery store, Granddad wouldn't tie the horse where there was no shade. Besides, his regu-

lar business was elsewhere. He waited with folded arms
on the seat while we unloaded the wagon. As Mama
climbed down, he looked back narrow-eyed at her. "Anything you want took to the post office?"

Mama walked along the wagon to him. Without a
word she pulled an envelope from her apron and handed
it up to him. Then she sailed past the hitching rail and
into the store.

Oh, the dim mysteries of Oldweilers' store—the coal
oil lamps burning through the day, the mingled salt and
sawdust scent, and sometimes in a keg, oysters I couldn't
imagine swallowing.

Buster tacked toward the penny candy jar. Mama
gathered her courage to do business with Mr. Oldweiler.
He looked relieved to be dealing with her and not
Granddad. That may have left him unprepared. Mama
wanted three cents more the dozen on eggs. And she had
him over a barrel with the butter. Nobody had better
butter than ours.

Lottie and I traded looks behind Mama's back. What
was she braving town to raise extra money for? said
Lottie's expression.

Mine replied: For Chicago. I told you were going. But
Lottie shook her head, sure that Mama had just now sent
the tickets back.

Mr. Oldweiler mopped his forehead with a blue ban-
danna. In doing business Mama was very ladylike, and
that made her harder to deal with.

"Blackberries, Mrs. Beckett?" he said. We hadn't sold him blackberries before. He reached for one and ate it, which was a point in our favor.

"The Almanac calls this a bad year for berries." Mama gazed sadly down at ours like they were the last.

Lottie popped her eyes at me. Mama didn't believe a word in the Farmer's Almanac. She said it was folklore.

When it was time to settle up, I'd never seen so much money change hands. "You can take out for a stick of candy," Mama said. Then Mr. Oldweiler gave us three for a penny. One for Buster and two for Lottie and me, just to see us blush.

Outside, Lottie found her voice first. "Well, Mama, you drive a hard bargain."

"It's not in my nature, though," Mama said quietly. "I'd sooner be home."

I thought we were headed there now. Mama would want to get this much money straight into her mattress. We began to stroll instead, our heels ringing on the wooden walk. Buster lagged behind.

We went by the hardware and turned our bonnets to the street past the barber shop. Mama surprised us by swerving into the dry goods. It was the biggest store in town and a different world from Oldweilers', though as dim and mysterious. Thin, high-collared women you never saw anywhere else worked in there. One sat in a cage at the back to take your money.

A dress dummy stopped us dead just inside. It wore a

stiff straw hat like one of Granddad's, with a grosgrain band. Its white shirtwaist was starchy and laid in flat pleats. Its belt buckle was two hands clasping. The gabardine skirt, a pale cream, just cleared the floor. The toes of the shoes came to perfect points, and they were snow white.

Lottie's shoes were black. Mine that had been hers were brown. We stood there in awe. I was still in short skirts, showing a length of leg between my high-top shoe and my skirt tails.

One of the women who worked there came forward. She wore a pencil in her bun, a tape measure around her neck, a pincushion on her wrist. She observed our sunbonnets.

"Is that what they're wearing now?" Mama said in a low voice, as if to spare the dress dummy's feelings.

The salesclerk nodded, looking away, though we were the only people in the place.

"That hat." Mama nodded at the dummy's head. "It's very mannish, isn't it?"

Mama didn't wear hats, but the one she was wearing in her mind right now had flowers on it. Lilacs, I expect, her favorite.

"Simplicity is the keynote this season," the saleswoman said.

"Then I take it that's why there's no machine lace on the collar of that shirtwaist."

The woman nodded. "Did you want to look through the pattern book?"

You bought very little ready-made in those days. You bought the yardage and you cut it out from a pattern at home. In your button box you already had plenty of buttons. I liked looking through the pattern book, though the outfits were always for occasions that never arose.

"The pattern book?" Mama said. "Indeed not. We haven't time to make anything up. Would an outfit like that do for the fair?" She was bolder about the dress dummy now, pointing right at it.

"The state fair?" the saleslady said, because our sunbonnets would do for that. "In Springfield?"

"Certainly not," said Mama, grander than I'd ever heard her be. "The Columbian Exposition at Chicago."

The wind went out of me. But now we knew, or thought we did. I'd been right: We were going to the fair. The letter Mama had handed to Granddad told Aunt Euterpe we were coming. The saleslady turned for a larger size in everything for Lottie, a smaller size for me.

My first thought was a big one. I'd be in long skirts at last. My skirt for the fair would brush my shoe tops, and there'd be no going back from that. I supposed there was wear left in the shoes we already had. But I saw Mama eye the dummy's polished pair, white for summertime. My heart jumped over the moon.

Now Mama turned back for Buster. He hung just inside the store, suspicious. The place was a quagmire of yardage on bolts, quilting frames, and a notions counter spiky with crochet hooks. Worse, corsets were laid out where you could see them. Buster shied from it all.

Mama summoned him. Another saleslady was called for. Come to find out, Buster needed knickerbocker britches, an Eton jacket, and a wide collar to his shirt, with a flowing, artistic black sateen cravat, and a sailor hat. And long black ribbed socks to go with new high-top shoes. His feet had grown a size since he'd last had shoes on.

Buster sagged.

Later, much later, we staggered outside, loaded like pack mules with paper parcels tied in twine. It was more Christmas than we'd ever had—in July. We were too stunned to gibber, and Buster was speechless with rage. Mama had spent all she'd gotten off Mr. Oldweiler and more she'd brought from home.

To our everlasting shame we hadn't given her a thought. "Mama," I said, "you didn't get anything for yourself."

"I've got plenty laid back I never get to wear," she said, looking away.

"Well, Mama," Lottie said, "you don't have white shoes."

"Yours won't be white long," Mama replied. "They say the Chicago streets are filthy as a hog wallow."

She turned us down the boardwalk. There we came upon Granddad staring in the window of the pharmacy.

We expected to be complained of for taking up so much of his valuable time. But he was drinking in a big poster showing a fine-looking man in a western hat.

In fancy letters the poster read:

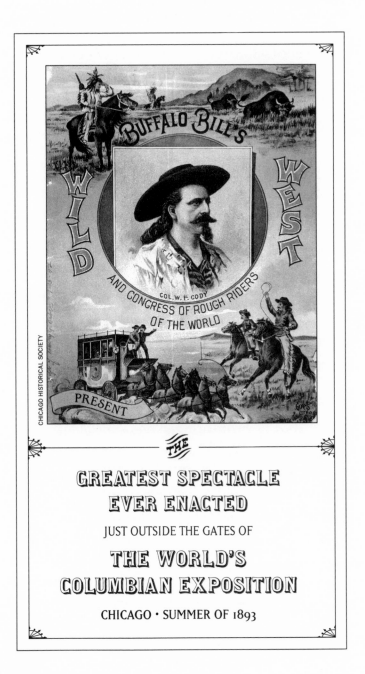

BUFFALO BILL'S

WILD WEST

COL. W. F. CODY

AND CONGRESS OF ROUGH RIDERS OF THE WORLD

PRESENT

THE

GREATEST SPECTACLE EVER ENACTED

JUST OUTSIDE THE GATES OF

THE WORLD'S COLUMBIAN EXPOSITION

CHICAGO · SUMMER OF 1893

Granddad's old eyes traced the colonel's every detail: the fringe on his buckskin coat, the elegant curve of his longhorn moustaches, and the tilt of his hat. Granddad was lost in admiration.

But when he sensed us there, he snorted. "That wasn't in no way how we dressed when we was settlin' this part of the country. All we had to wear was denim britches put together with rivets. And—"

"We was happy to have them," we all chanted under our breath.

But Granddad could hardly tear his eyes away from the poster, though he was ready for home. We walked a good long way to where he'd tied Lillian to a shade tree. Granddad didn't deign to remark on all our parcels. You were never sure what he noticed. But he saw the black cloud hanging over Buster.

After he'd turned the horse in the street, he called back to him. "Boy, climb up here and ride shotgun for me and Tip."

So Buster tramped past us and hauled himself up between Granddad and Tip. We were in open country when we heard Granddad say, "What's got stuck in your craw?"

Sulky, Buster said, "They've tricked me out like a circus pony. They want me to wear a thing around my neck like a girl's."

Granddad looked down at Buster over his specs. "Women," he said.

"I ain't going to wear any of it," Buster declared.

Granddad considered. "Well, boy, you can't go nekkid in Chicago. The wind comes right off the lake."

Then he handed Buster the reins, and Lillian Russell took us home, jaunty all the way under the blue dome of heaven.

FASTER THAN A
GALLOPING HORSE

⚬━━━━━⚬

For a week we worked like beavers to make up for the time we'd be away. We put up peas and beans. We cooked down enough berry preserves and strained enough jelly to see us through to the Second Coming. The sticker scratches glowed on my arms.

A pan of melting wax was always at the back of the stove, for sealing the jam jars. We'd have pickled peaches if we could have talked them into ripening in time.

We were still at it by lamplight every night. Then Wednesday came around, and Mama wanted us out of the kitchen before Everett came to call on Lottie. He was never invited over the threshold, but Mama was particular about us clearing out of the kitchen. It was hard to fathom her thoughts. Maybe she didn't want him to think we were spying on him.

I was in the porch swing when Lottie came out wearing her new white shoes under the fresh apron she always put on for Everett. She said she was breaking in the shoes. She was showing them off to see if he'd notice.

Then right away there he came, all over the road, so I went on in the house. As I made my way through the darkened front room, I fell over Mama.

"Hush," she whispered. She was bent to the window, watching Everett trying to turn the wagon into the lane. She was spying, if you ask me. If Buster was under the porch, we made quite a crowd.

"Did you notice how pale and spindly he was earlier in the summer before the sun got to him?" Mama said in my ear.

Even in the evening at a distance he had a better color. And he was looking broader across the shoulders from heavy work. He was not bad-looking, though I didn't point this out to Mama.

"I have an idea he's been in jail," she whispered. "That's why he was so pale. They get that way."

My land, I thought.

"But he's a talker," Mama murmured. That was true. We didn't know what they found to talk about. But we could hear the mumble of their voices every Wednesday night, and he did more than his share. He'd bring a book sometimes and read it to Lottie.

"I hope it's not the Bible," Mama remarked, "because I have a feeling he's not a Methodist."

But I didn't think it was a revival meeting Lottie and Everett were conducting out there on the porch.

Mama muttered, not for the first time, "We don't know a thing about him."

"I guess we could ask," I said, being pert.

"I'd sooner nip this in the bud," said Mama.

On the night before we were to leave, Lottie and I sat upright in the bed like birds on a branch. Our new get-ups were laid out around the room. We were to wear them to make a good impression on Aunt Euterpe, if such a thing was possible. At the foot of the bed were two egg crates packed with the rest. We had nothing resembling valises.

We were all set to go. We were cocked and primed. But something fearful was coming over me. I had some shyness in me that may have come from Mama. Of course, at that age I didn't know *what* I was, because I had a history of spunkiness too. And a scrap or two in the schoolyard to prove it, in years past. I'd even gone on the stage once, for a minute.

They were having a school program where the families came. Lottie had tricked me out in a costume and made me memorize a song. I couldn't have been more than six, and too dumb to fight her about it. They pushed me onto the stage, and I held out my skirts and sang:

When first I stepped upon the stage,
My heart went pitty-pat,
And I thought I heard somebody say,
"What little fool is that?"

That was all of the song I could remember, so I naturally burst into tears and had to be led off. It would be many a year before I sang another solo.

Now I wondered if that school program had marked me for life, because flouncing off to Chicago liked to scare me out of my skin. Staying tucked in right here at home, safe from a world full of complete strangers, began to look good.

The lamp burned beside Lottie, and she was staring into space. We supposed we were too tired to sleep. In fact, we were worried to death. *I* was.

Even so, I couldn't leave Lottie be for long. I began to pluck the petals off an imaginary daisy, chanting:

He loves me,
He don't.
He'll have me,
He won't.
He would if he could,
But he can't.

"Be quiet, Rosie," Lottie said.

"What do you and Everett find to talk about?" I inquired.

"This and that," she said. "Nothing to concern you."

"Mama says Everett's very probably been in jail."

"He says he feels like he has been," Lottie answered unexpectedly.

"Mama says she wants to nip—"

The door to the hall moved. We thought of Buster. It opened, and Mama slipped into the room, barefoot in her nightdress. Though it wasn't but nine o'clock, she put a finger to her lips as if the world was asleep. Her hair was loose around her face. You hardly saw the streak of white. She drew nigh us, throwing her shadow on the wall. Then she edged onto the bed, my side. We gazed at her, waiting.

She cleared her throat. ". . . Your aunt Euterpe was always particular, you know," she said, speaking low. We listened for more.

". . . And she's kind of prissy, there's no doubt about it. She always carried a long-stemmed rose in her teeth to the privy, to cut the smell."

We stared.

"And she can be stiff-necked," Mama said. "You're to play by her rules. Remember, she never had children, so you're all apt to come as a shock to her."

"Mama, don't tell us we're to spend the whole time up in Chicago trying to keep track of Buster," Lottie said.

"I don't worry so much about Buster as I do about you two," Mama answered. "Give me boys anytime. You know where you stand with boys."

"Well, Mama," says Lottie, "if we step out of line, you can jerk knots in our tails."

A silence dropped on us. Quieter than before Mama said, "No, I can't. I'm not going."

My heart stopped. Time stopped. Lottie nearly nudged a hole in me. She'd known right along. Our two new straw hats with the grosgrain bands, mannish but lady-like, hung from the rocker. Where would we wear them now? Suddenly I wanted to go, like anything.

"I sent my ticket back to Euterpe and told her to meet the three of you at the station up there without fail," Mama said.

We were going by ourselves? I liked to have fainted.

"Mama!" Lottie slapped the sheet. "You're sending us off on our own?"

"I don't like to." Mama looked away at the wall. "I won't draw an easy breath till I get you back."

"Does Dad want you home?" Lottie demanded.

"He wants me to go with you," Mama said, whisper quiet.

"Then, Mama," I said, "why don't you?"

"Oh, mercy. How could I get away at this time of year?" she said. "Can you picture your granddad playing milkmaid? He'd spill the cream and break the churn. You go on to Chicago and see the fair, then come back and tell me all about it."

She said no more, so I spoke up. "Mama, are you scared to go?"

Lottie grabbed my hand and squeezed it to shut me up, though Mama could see. Then, very soft for her, Lottie said, "Mama, we'll look at everything twice, once for you."

Mama turned away with her chin tucked down. Then she was gone. We didn't think we'd sleep a wink. We slept like logs.

Then, as in a storybook, it was tomorrow. In the dazzling morning we were on the train, perched at the edge of the slick wicker seats in the chair car. The awful roar of the locomotive pulling into the depot had silenced our good-byes, which was just as well.

Our picnic hamper was at our feet. Our hearts were in our mouths. We gazed out at Mama and Dad alone down there on the platform. The window was half open, but we couldn't think of anything to say. We sensed the locomotive pawing the track, mad to move on.

At the last moment Buster sprang from his seat and swarmed up the aisle. As the conductor lifted the metal step, Buster leaned out the door of our car and flung his sailor hat. The locomotive released steam, carrying the hat down the platform. I hoped Mama would get it and return it to the store.

With an awful jolt we were off. Mama and Dad slid away from the window. Dad's arm reached around Mama's shoulders.

I'd never gone faster than a horse gallops. We braced ourselves for speed as the town fell away. But before Lottie got Buster settled in the seat opposite, the train was shuddering to a halt. The brakes squealed, and so did we. This must be the Bulldog Crossing, but then the train lit out running and flung itself down the tracks.

Soot billowed in the window, and we caught a familiar smell. A farmer was dragging a creosote-soaked log around a wheat field to repel the army worms. That was our last whiff of home.

To save our skirts Lottie and I had brought tea towels hemmed out of feed sacks to sit on. As Mama said, you didn't know who'd sat down there before you. We skidded on the slippery seat, scared we'd disgrace ourselves by sliding onto the floor. We jiggled, and I happened to notice that Buster's pocket jumped.

We knew to keep our tickets handy for the conductor to punch. The door at the end of our car opened, and I held up my ticket to show I knew how to act. But the man staggering through the door wasn't the conductor. It was another man entirely, in a once-cream-colored suit, badly creased, and a curly-brimmed Panama hat, a high celluloid collar, and a silk cravat. A bachelor button hung in his lapel. Lottie gasped. I skidded off the seat and she caught me in midair.

The old geezer scanned the car over his pushed-down spectacles. His crepy neck hung down in dewlaps over the unfamiliar collar. His knobby old hands clutched the chair backs as he worked his way along the car, ducking the kerosene lamps swinging overhead.

"Hey, it's Granddad!" Buster sang out, turning to see.

Lottie and I slumped.

FLYING TO THE MOON

Buster grinned from ear to ear. In Mama's own voice Lottie said, "Granddad, what in tunket are you doing on this train?"

He scooted Buster over and sat. From nowhere he flourished forth a rustic walking stick and planted both hands on it. "I'm goin' to the fair, same as you. Had to flag the train at the Bulldog Crossing."

"You're going all the way to the fair with us, Granddad?" Buster beamed. Granddad had evened up the sides between girls and boys in Buster's opinion.

"I want to take in the livestock display," Granddad said, mostly around his chaw. "They've got Eye-talian gondolas too, and I'm thinkin' about having a boat ride in one. Might even take a turn on the big wheel. I'm studyin' several things I plan to do."

Lottie sighed. "Granddad, where'd you get the train ticket?"

"I'm ridin' on your maw's," he said. "She was sending it back, and I didn't want it to go to waste. Your maw'll be easier in her mind if she knows I'm along to look after you young'uns."

We young'uns gaped.

Lottie pressed on. "Granddad, how did you come by Mama's ticket?"

Granddad gazed down the aisle. "When your maw handed me the letter for Euterpe, it felt like there was a ticket inside."

"You tore open the envelope and took it out?" Lottie accused.

"I was careful," Granddad said in his own defense. "I gummed the flap back before I turned it in at the post office."

"What did Mama think about that?"

"She don't know yet. I left her a note in the kitchen, so my absence won't worry her."

"And does Aunt Euterpe know you're coming?"

"It'll be a surprise for her," Granddad said.

And we all agreed to that. Lottie sat back, murmuring, "As if Buster wasn't going to be trouble enough . . ."

"Granddad," Buster piped up, "where'd you get them clothes?"

Even the people across the aisle must have wondered. Granddad stuck out a mile in that old ice-cream suit, fly-specked with rust spots. He looked like a riverboat gambler down on his luck.

"These is my traveling togs," he explained with quiet pride.

"Where'd you ever go?" Buster wondered.

"Go? I'm a rolling stone, boy. I wore this out to St. Joseph, Missouri, here a while back."

"What for?" Buster kicked his new heels.

Granddad stared down at him. "Same reason anybody goes to St. Joe. To see the house where they shot Jesse James. The bullet went clean through his skull and lodged in the wall. I wanted to see that and poke my finger in the bullet hole. It's just something you do if you're an American."

Everybody in the car could hear him. Lottie was mortified. The ticket was limp in my hand before the conductor came around to punch it. He was a big red-faced man in a blue uniform and a braided cap. He gave Granddad a second look.

"Well, old timer," the conductor said, "how you doing?"

Granddad looked up suspiciously. "Can't complain." He fished for Mama's ticket in his waistcoat. "Of course, my needs is simple." Then Granddad spoke out, full-voiced:

Beefsteak when I'm hongry,
Corn likker when I'm dry,

Pretty little gal when I'm lonesome,
Sweet heaven when I die.

The lady across the aisle lowered her veil suddenly. When the conductor recovered, he said, "I see by your ticket you're traveling through to Chicago."

Granddad agreed and pointed us out. "These is my grandkids." Lottie looked way too old to be riding on a child's ticket, but Granddad had distracted the conductor. "I'm takin' these young'uns to see the fair. They's green as gourds and never seen nothing. I'm going to show them the sights."

"Well, sir," said the conductor, moving on, "when you get to Chicago, there'll be another sight to see."

We sat at the big depot in Decatur while more people got on. Then we were up and running again. Granddad eyed the picnic hamper. I didn't know if I could eat anything at this speed. But we laid out a picnic lunch with the big checked napkins over our knees. Of course there was plenty.

A fried chicken had lost its head but yesterday when Lottie picked it out specially and wrung its neck off. To fill in we had sandwiches stuffed with ham smoked in our own smokehouse over green–apple tree wood. And an applesauce spice cake we could eat with our fingers and a jug of sun tea to wash it down.

"Eat hearty," said Granddad with his mouth full. "You

never know what kind of day-old slop people have to eat in Chicago. And I'll tell you one thing for free. Your aunt Euterpe can't no more cook than she can fly to the moon."

But I thought we were flying to the moon this minute—eating a picnic lunch on a speeding train. And Chicago getting closer and closer, over the curve of the earth.

Then keyed up though we were, we all took naps. Granddad went first. His Panama was on his lap, and his stick clattered to the floor. His head lolled back, and he was asleep at the top of his lungs. Buster's eyelids got droopier than his socks. Then he was dozing in the crook of Granddad's arm. Lottie went next, though upright with her hat on. I thought I'd better stay alert for us all, and dropped right off.

So imagine our dismay when the train set its brakes, and Lottie and I both shot off our seat and onto the floor. Down on our hands and knees with Granddad's stick. But now he was dragging us up. We were indoors some-place. We were in the great cavern of the station—there already. I could have wailed with fear.

But there wasn't time for that. We pulled down our egg crates from overhead. Everybody in the car was surging for the door. It was all too soon.

We stepped straight out onto a concrete platform thronged with people filing in the same direction. As we approached the waiting room, Granddad dropped back.

"You kids go on," he said. "I have business in the baggage car."

So there we were, dragged down by our crates and alone in the world.

"A fat lot of good Granddad'll be to us," Lottie said in a shaking voice. We were swept forward, keeping Buster between us. I nearly tangled in my new long skirt. The elastic that held on my new straw hat cut into my chin. You couldn't see a step ahead, or a minute, and there was nothing to breathe but smoke.

The crowds parted, and over there under a clock stood a woman. She was all in black, even the gloves in this stifling afternoon. The feathers on her veiled hat were stumpy raven's wings. She was either the Angel of Death or Aunt Euterpe.

We drew nearer her. She reached up and propped her veil back over her hat.

"Adelaide," she cried softly, reaching for Lottie. "Oh, Adelaide, you came after all."

Adelaide was Mama's name. Dad called her Addy. Aunt Euterpe thought Lottie was Mama.

"I'm Lottie," Lottie squeaked.

Aunt Euterpe's hands flew to her long pale face. She was a wan woman, nothing like Mama. She wore spectacles on a chain, and her eyes were bewildered behind them.

"I'm Rosie," I said to help her out. "This here is Buster."

"Yes, it would be." Aunt Euterpe spoke faintly. "But you're all so . . . big."

"Granddad says we're overgrown," I told her.

Aunt Euterpe started suddenly like a goose had walked over her grave. She stared past us, evidently seeing a ghost. I took that to be Granddad himself.

When we turned, he had a surprise for us too. In his hands was a leash. Straining at the end of it was Tip.

"Granddad!" Buster burst out. "You brought Tip!" Buster was tickled pink.

"He pines and gets off his feed if I leave him behind." Granddad dodged Aunt Euterpe's stricken stare.

"Papa," she said, this sad greeting rising from her flat bosom.

"Hello there, Terpie," he croaked. "I rode your sister's ticket up here to keep an eye on these children. Me and Tip."

"I see," she said regretfully. Compressing her lips in martyrdom, she lowered her veil. We followed her out through a great stone arch to the teeming street.

A polished black carriage stood tall in a line of hacks. Aunt Euterpe pointed us at the open door. Granddad gave Tip's haunches a boost up. We milled around inside—hats and veils, elbows and paws, Granddad's stick. While we settled, the driver tied our crates to the roof.

"Land-a-Goshen, you're spreadin' your money around, girl," Granddad said to Aunt Euterpe. He was impressed in spite of himself. You couldn't hire a rig like this from the livery stable down home. The carriage had brass side lamps and leather straps to lower the windows. A cut-glass vase hung beside the buttoned seat with a single red rose in it.

"I feel like a pallbearer at my own funeral," said Granddad as Buster settled on his knee.

"I could hardly get you all onto the streetcar with all your . . . luggage. Even before I knew about the . . . animal." Aunt Euterpe spoke from behind her veil. I'd already forgotten what she looked like.

We were in a procession of carriages and beer wagons. The street was laid in granite blocks, and we'd never ridden on paving before. We seemed to float. The city clattered and cried out around us. Granddad stuck his head out the window to see to the top of a building. Buster and Tip too.

"It is the Masonic Temple," Aunt Euterpe murmured, "the tallest building in the world." So we were on State Street now.

"How high is it?" Buster wondered.

"Twenty-two stories," Aunt Euterpe said.

Granddad pulled his head back inside right quick like the building might fall on him.

Bells rang when we came to an iron bridge swinging open to let a big boat through. You couldn't see the river till you were right up on it for everything in the way. A peacock's tail of scummy grease spread over the river water. The smell would have knocked you off your perch. I didn't like to think what all those things floating in the stream might be. Mama had been right: Chicago was filthy as a hog wallow.

We turned at a stone water tower, and by and by on our right was Lake Michigan sweeping flat and blue to the far edge of the world. On the other side of the road rose one palace after another.

Granddad stared. "Is them houses?" They were big as towns, gated like graveyards.

"Private residences," Aunt Euterpe said. "We have just passed the Franklin McVeahs'. We are now approaching the Potter Palmers'. Mrs. Potter Palmer is the President of the Board of Lady Managers for the fair." There was longing in Aunt Euterpe's voice, but I didn't know what it meant.

We turned at last into a narrower street, tree-lined. It was Schiller Street, and we'd never known anybody who lived on a road with a name. Here too the houses were fine, though run together in rows. We drew up with a jangle.

"This where you hang your hat, Terpie?" Granddad inquired.

"In a manner of speaking," Aunt Euterpe replied.

The driver dropped from the box to help us down. Tip went first in a great leap to the nearest tree.

When Granddad's turn came, he creaked down un-aided. He didn't like the look of the driver in his bulging black suit and derby hat to match. You wouldn't want to meet up with him in a dark alley. He hustled our crates up the steps. At the top a maid in a frilly cap stood before double doors.

Not wanting to be robbed, Granddad clutched his carpetbag. "You cain't be too careful in such territory as this," he muttered, though the man was driving the carriage away now.

"The driver is my servant," Aunt Euterpe said. "That was my carriage."

A solitary feather would have knocked us all down. Granddad's old eyes expanded in his specs. He gaped up at the house, elegant with stonework and bay windows. It rose like the Masonic Temple.

"You don't mean to tell me you live in this whole house, Terpie?" he said.

"I do," said Aunt Euterpe, muffled by veils. "In the solitude of my grief."

Granddad scratched up under his Panama. "Heckatee, Terpie," he said. "You're settin' pretty."

Lottie sagged against me. We'd never known anybody rich, and our aunt was. The cat had our tongues, though Buster was telling Tip that up here he couldn't just roam around like he owned the place the way he did down home. Not in Chicago he couldn't.

BRIGHT LIGHTS AND BAD WOMEN

⌘

E vening shadows found us clustered at the dining-
room table. Aunt Euterpe's huge, unexplored house
hulked over us. She hadn't brought electrical wire into it
because, as she said, she didn't understand how electricity
worked. Blue flame flickered from the gasolier above our
heads, making us all look long dead.

We hadn't changed our clothes, as we were already
wearing our best. In his ice-cream suit Granddad glowed.
Aunt Euterpe had unveiled herself for dinner and drooped
at her place like a waxen lily. Timidly she tinkled a tar-
nished bell beside her plate.

The door fanned open, and in came a woman backward, bearing plates of soup—a big, husky woman in a

cook's cap. She looked like she might butcher cattle on her day off. Behind her with more plates was the maid who'd let us in. What a lot of people it took to keep Aunt Euterpe going.

When the big cook skidded the soup plates under our noses, Granddad stared down through his specs. It was a mighty thin soup. You could see the roses on the bottom of the plate. Greasy too, with things floating in it. I was reminded of the Chicago River.

Granddad was not a swearing man, not in front of women and children. But Mama allowed him two oaths in the house. One was hecka-tee. The other was helaca-toot.

"Helaca-toot, Terpie!" he cried out. "What kind of excuse for soup is this? It looks like somethin' drained out of the umbrella stand."

The little maid shied. The big cook glared at Granddad and barged back to the kitchen.

"Oh, Papa," Aunt Euterpe whispered.

Though he'd only sampled the soup, Granddad wrung out his moustache and waited for the next course. We all dreaded it, and with good reason. It was boiled mutton and two tough cabbage leaves. Peeping out from under the cabbage were the many eyes of a gray potato. Aunt Euterpe took up her fork in a hopeful way, but Granddad flung back in his chair.

"I'd sooner eat a pan-fried overshoe!" He folded his arms in that stubborn way he had. So did Buster. It was a

worry to us how Buster learned his manners from Granddad.

The cook had been listening behind the door. Now
she was back, looming over Aunt Euterpe. "Lissen, Miz
Fleischacker," she thundered. "I ain't used to having my
cookery bad-mouthed, especially by some old hayseed
of a—"

"Yes, Mrs. O'Shay," Aunt Euterpe murmured. "It is
only a misunderstanding."

The little maid peering around the door vanished
when Mrs. O'Shay banged through it.

Lottie shot me a look, and I read it plain. Aunt
Euterpe was afraid of her hired help.

Dessert was stewed prunes, and that did it for Granddad. He threw his napkin and pushed back his chair. "I
have an idee they're eatin' better than this over at the fairgrounds."

"Papa! You can't think of going to the fair tonight."
Aunt Euterpe spoke from behind a napkin pressed to her
lips.

"Why not? They'd have the lights on."

"I can't ask Flanagan to bring the carriage around
again." Aunt Euterpe quivered. "He wouldn't like it."

When Granddad's dander was up, his chin looked like
a clenched fist. "Then how do the common people get to
the fair?"

Aunt Euterpe swayed in her chair. "The Illinois Central runs cars down to the gate. But, Papa, it's getting late.

You couldn't possibly take these children. Awful, rough types come out after dark. And bad . . . women."

Bright lights and bad women were no discouragement to Granddad. We were on our way to the fair before we knew. And Aunt Euterpe too, for fear we children would all be murdered and Mama would hold it against her.

We took our second trip by train in a single day. The Illinois Central blazed like a meteor across Chicago, flashing past the lighted windows of people who never looked up. And crowded? It was a regular cattle car. We had to stand up, cheek-by-jowl with perfect strangers, though people stepped aside from Aunt Euterpe's many black veils. Others drew back for a look at Granddad in his finery. But did any man get up to give Aunt Euterpe his seat? Not in Chicago he didn't.

We clung to leather nooses that hung from the ceiling of the car. Lottie and I kept Buster between us. We were worn to a frazzle before we were halfway there. But then we pulled into the cavern of another vast station, this one built expressly for the fair. A human tidal wave swept us through the turnstiles. Ahead of us looked like daybreak. The whole sky was on fire.

Onward we went, and how can I explain how it was to us? There was no night. White electricity had lit the world and erased the stars. Now we were standing beside a long body of water, busy with drifting gondolas. On both sides of the pond stood the great pavilions of the

Columbian Exposition, the White City. It was Greece and Rome again, and every column and curlicue lit by an incandescent bulb.

On either side of us plumes of water danced in every hollyhock color. There in the square lake ahead a stone replica of a ship pretended to float. It may have been like the one Christopher Columbus sailed into the New World, sent on his way by Spanish royalty.

We couldn't take it in. We couldn't breathe. Granddad whispered, "Hecka-tee, Edison. What have you done?"

"This is the Court of Honor," Aunt Euterpe said. It shimmered all the way to a pier out into Lake Michigan. "It is one corner of the fair."

"There's more?" There couldn't be.

"Six hundred acres." She pointed out the great Halls of Machinery and Agriculture and Mines, the Hall of Music and the Casino, all of them doubled by the reflecting pool. From the roof of the Hall of Electricity the Westinghouse alternating-current searchlight swept the scene in a terrifying way.

Lottie had my hand in a grip of steel. We hadn't bargained on anything like this. We were scared, of course, but I longed to be a poet, to pin this vision to a page. It had a beauty beyond your wildest dreams, and so big, it made us mice.

It was too much world for me all at once, and I heard Lottie thinking the same. The music of a full brass band playing "The Columbian March" wavered over the summer-thunder sound of all this multitude of people. My eyes stung.

"Granddad," Buster said, "I'm hungry."

Dragging Buster, we drifted in this dream among the crowds. Like Venice, the fair was built on canals, arched with marble bridges. We walked forever beside the Manufacturers Hall. There across more water rose the great cut-glass dome of the Horticultural Building. On an island against the fiery night were the strange swooping roofs of the Japanese village. People moved around us in trances like ours, feeling the light on their faces. Ladies in gondolas trailed their hands in the bright water.

"Where can a fella get some grub?" Granddad called out to all in earshot. "I thought Chicago was a German town. Where's the schnitzel?"

Aunt Euterpe quaked.

A man who didn't know Granddad from Adam turned to say, "Well, old sport, they want an arm and a leg for eats here on the grounds. Try the Midway."

Aunt Euterpe lurched. She grabbed at both us girls.

"What's the Midway, Aunt Euterpe?" Lottie asked.

"It is a sinkhole of corruption," she murmured, low and hopeless. "I made a solemn vow to keep you children clear of it. No decent—"

"Is it where the Ferris wheel is?" Buster piped up. He was always right there when you didn't want him to hear.

"Anybody know where the Midway is?" Granddad called out. People began to point the way.

We led Aunt Euterpe, and she wasn't herself. "If only I hadn't written that letter to your mother," she was mumbling. "What a can of worms I have opened."

But Lottie gripped her elbow. "Never mind, Aunt Euterpe. If the Midway isn't for decent people, you won't see anybody you know." It looked like Lottie was taking charge. "And throw back your veils, Aunty," she said, "or you'll miss your footing on all these marble steps." Lottie was firm with her.

We found the Midway. We had two fine bridges to cross. Then past the great dome of the Illinois Building and behind the Woman's Building, the White City stopped. We left the exposition and ganged with the thickening crowds under the Illinois Central tracks. Then there it was, bellowing music and blazing in lights of every color. The Midway—the Midway Plaisance, to give its proper name.

We'd left the white marble and fine statues behind us. This was another world. Here was Hagenback's Animal Show featuring bears on bicycles. Here was the Blarney Castle in an Irish village pounding with clog dancers. The Persians were here, and the Javanese and the Congress of International Beauties. Music came from every direction until I thought my ears would drown. There were calliopes and tambourines and the beat of the cannibal drum. Up on a stage at an upright piano a young man named Scott Joplin banged out tunes you could hear with your feet.

On both sides of the Midway the world had come to strut its stuff: an ostrich farm and the Turkish Village and the Panorama of the Bernese Alps. There was an ice rink here in the depth of summer, and everything lit up like a Christmas tree.

The sweetness of taffy pulled on giant machines hung in the air. Corn on the cob boiled in giant vats. Sausage was being fried with onions, though you could tell from here the lard wasn't fresh.

Granddad parted the common people with his stick, and we clung like leeches to him. One false step, and the crowds would swallow you like Jonah's whale.

Then I looked up and staggered back. Ahead of us in the center of the Midway was the fright of my life. It was the giant wheel. We were walking straight toward it. You couldn't see to the top of the thing. It rose into the night. The creak of its struts and girders sounded in my dreams for years.

Granddad himself drew up and threw back his head. People rode the wheel in thirty-six cars. While they weren't quite as big as railroad cars, they'd hold sixty people each. To see them moving up there in the night air was beyond anything.

"They say the axle on that thing is forty-five foot

across," Granddad explained. "The largest single hunk of steel ever forged." But he spoke in a hushed and strangely respectful voice.

"We ain't a-going to ride it tonight, are we?" Buster asked. Whenever he was scared, his grammar got worse.

"I thought you was hungry," said Granddad to spare him.

In front of a place called Old Vienna people ate out in the open. A waiter was settling us around a table when Aunt Euterpe leapt up like she'd sat on an anthill. "Girls, don't look!" she shrieked, reaching for our eyes.

My land, I thought. Did somebody fall off the Ferris wheel? Naturally, we looked. Just across the Midway was a vast cardboard place with minarets. It was called A Street in Cairo. A big sign offered camel rides, if you can imagine wanting to do that. It was a popular spot. Throngs were going inside.

"Papa!" Aunt Euterpe said. "We can't stay here. We must leave at once."

Granddad hunkered down in his chair. "I don't budge till I bin fed and watered." But now he too was looking over at A Street in Cairo. "Is this where that girl called Little Egypt does her dance?" he inquired.

Aunt Euterpe crumpled. A musical clatter of bells wafted across the Midway. Four women wearing veils far thinner than Aunt Euterpe's—and very little else—capered on a stage and did a dance like you never saw. They flung their hips to the four winds, and there were bells on their toes.

Aunt Euterpe was near tears, and Granddad was all eyes. "Hecka-tee," he whispered.

We had us a good supper at the Old Vienna, though Granddad warned us not to order the bratwurst.

"Chicago's a meat-packin' town," he explained, "and once in a while a workin' man will fall into the grinder and come out as links of prime smoked sausage."

Lottie swallowed hard.

But we made a hearty meal out of sauerbraten, sour potato salad, and vinegared cucumbers. Over our heads the terrible wheel creaked. Across the Midway dancing girls writhed like serpents. It liked to kill Aunt Euterpe, but Lottie told her, "Aunty, they're doing Salome's dance of the seven veils. It's from the Bible. Eat your supper."

In time Aunt Euterpe licked her platter clean like she couldn't remember her last square meal. Maybe she couldn't. We all ate like thrashers, Granddad missing his mouth several times from watching the dancers.

They didn't let Little Egypt out on the stage. To see her dance, you had to pay and go inside. They charged you every time you turned around at the fair. They just about charged you to breathe.

We hadn't eaten this late in our lives, and we were full to the gills when we left Old Vienna. The Midway was seven eighths of a mile long, and we'd only traversed half of it. The crowds swept us along by a big pink-lit structure called The Columbian Theater.

Buster bounced and pointed up. "Granddad! You brought Lillian!"

To our wondering eyes a big sign over the theater spelled out in electric bulbs:

```
PRESENTING THE
TOAST OF AMERICA
LILLIAN RUSSELL
```

I didn't know what to think. It wasn't beyond Granddad to bring his horse to Chicago. He'd brought Tip. But nobody would call Granddad's old gray mare the toast of America. Aunt Euterpe snatched at Lottie and me.

Granddad stared open-mouthed up at the sign. Over the din of the crowd I could swear I heard him whisper, "My prayers is answered."

We got it sorted out. Lillian Russell—the real one—was a woman, an actress. Admiring her, Granddad had named his horse for her. It was the kind of thing he'd do.

"Papa!" Aunt Euterpe barked. "Don't think of taking these children to see that woman!" Aunt Euterpe's patience hung by a thread.

Granddad rounded on her. "Would it mark 'em for

life to see the prettiest gal and the sweetest singer in the United States?"

"She paints her face!" Aunt Euterpe shot back.

"So does Buffalo Bill," Granddad answered. "Girl, they're in *show business.*"

"Papa, she was barred from the Washington Park clubhouse by the best ladies in Chicago society!"

"They's hypocrites," Granddad spat.

"She's a fallen woman." Aunt Euterpe stumbled over her words.

"Horsefeathers," Granddad replied. "She's from Clinton, Iowa. And she can hit high C eight times in the same song."

"Papa," Aunt Euterpe reasoned hopelessly, "that woman has been married three times."

"She could marry four times if she'd have me!" The crowds around us stared at Granddad, and Lottie went beet red. "I'm goin' in to see the show," he said.

"Papa, I am taking these children home." Aunt Euterpe's patience had snapped.

"Take 'em," Granddad said, walking away already, following the crowds into The Columbian Theater.

Confused, Buster called after him, "Granddad, did you bring Lillian or not?"

Dear Mama and Dad,
    The Midway on our
first night! You never
saw such a sight.
    Your loving daughter,
        Rosie
P.S. We have Granddad.

POST CARD

6 PM
189_

1¢
UNITED STATES
POSTAGE

Mr. and Mrs.
    Gideon Beckett
Rural Christian
            County
    Illinois

THE WORST DAY IN AUNT EUTERPE'S LIFE

Part One

Somehow Aunt Euterpe found our way home to Schiller Street. It must have been midnight before Lottie and I climbed into the unfamiliar bed. Then she sat up, writing a letter to Mama and Dad. I dashed off a postcard, but she wanted to get everything down before something else happened. Whether she wrote to Everett or not I couldn't tell, and she didn't say.

I was almost off in dreamland when we heard Grand-dad's stumble on the stairs. He was singing a song, more or less. It was a new one to me. He must have picked it up on the Midway:

I ride alone to the distant blue,
My bicycle gliding away
To the fields of green
Where my loved one lies,
Awaiting the judgment day.

Then we slept, and awoke with a jolt. Daylight streamed in. We didn't know where we were at first. The bedroom, high in the house, was far smaller than our room down home: coffin-narrow and tall with a good deal of mahogany woodwork. The wallpaper was brown vines of ivy. The window was layered with curtains. The breeze was off the stockyards.

Lottie rose up like Lazarus beside me. "Rosie! We've overslept, and on our first day." Her substantial feet hit the floor. Her hair was a rat's nest. "There's a clock on the landing." She elbowed me out of the bed. "Go out there and see what time it is."

"It's pretty nearly five-thirty," I said, rushing back. We'd lolled in the bed like a pair of lazy town girls. Lottie was already pulling her underskirts up beneath her nightgown, grunting with the effort.

Aunt Euterpe's house had a bathroom lined with tile and bright with nickel fittings. We didn't tarry to marvel at it. Lottie didn't approve of the arrangements anyway. She said it wasn't sanitary to have the privy that near the sink.

But we were glad for the running water. Then she nearly scalped me by jerking my hair into quick, tight braids.

"Pin them up. I don't want them hanging down my back," I told her, but she claimed there wasn't time.

I'd brought a faded calico shirtwaist and a feed sack skirt for every day—a short skirt, sadly. In our old shoes we clattered down the hall past the door of Granddad and Buster's room, where they seemed dead to the world.

To our relief no one was in the kitchen before us. It was a dim room, and Tip whined at the back door like a lost soul. We handed out a mouthful of cold mutton for him, and he buried it in the yard. Lottie and I had found aprons and set to work.

We'd brought a double dozen eggs from home, now only a day old. An icebox stood in one corner with a pan beneath to catch the drips. Lottie rooted around in it for butter. I built up the fire in the range from stove lengths in a box. I knew that when Lottie got a good look at the stove, she'd hit the ceiling.

She did. "Rosie, we can't cook in here. The place is a pigsty."

It was. Nobody had cleaned that range since Grant took Richmond. The whole kitchen was a disgrace, crusted with old grease. We stuck to the floor with every step we took. And cobwebs? Everywhere you looked, like a haunted house.

We stacked the chairs on the table, drew a bucket of water and made suds, tied up our skirts, and fell to it. I laid into the floor with a scrub brush. The kitchen clock struck six as we began. It struck seven as we threw the last pail of black water out in the yard. But we'd lost all track of time.

Now we could get to breakfast, though we were wringing wet. I wondered if there was a slice of ham to go with the eggs, but Lottie said she'd trust nothing in this kitchen that had ever been alive. She told me to beat up a bowl of pancake batter if there were no weevils in the flour. She began cracking our eggs. Lottie never looked more like Mama than when she was standing over a skillet with a spatula in her hand.

To keep up the pace we began to sing, softly, falling back on the old chestnuts we'd sing down home:

I gambled in the game of love,
I played my heart and lost,
I'm now a wreck upon life's sea,
I fell and paid the cost

and

My mother was a lady,
Like yours, you will allow,
And you may have a sister
Who needs protection now.

Songs like those, and I took my cue from Lottie. Was I beginning to know I couldn't always take my cues from her?

With a bang like gunfire the door flung back, and there stood Mrs. O'Shay with blood in her eye.

Her hands were on her heavy hips. The very combs propping up her hair vibrated in outrage. "What do you two think you're doin' in my kitchen, if you wouldn't mind telling me?" she bellowed like she was calling hogs.

We nearly jumped out of our drawers. Around Mrs. O'Shay the little maid Bridget peered. Drifting up behind them like the ghost of herself was Aunt Euterpe. She wore a black shirtwaist and a human-hair brooch at her throat. "Oh, dear," she murmured, seeing me stacking cakes and Lottie looking for the coffee grinder.

"We were just pitching in to fix breakfast," Lottie said.

"We overslept," I mumbled, to explain.

Mrs. O'Shay whipped around and stuck her face into Aunt Euterpe's. "They got no business in my kitchen!" she hollered. "Don't they think I can cook?"

Wisely, we held our tongues. Aunt Euterpe went paler. "I am sure it was only a misunderstanding."

It commenced to dawn on us what we'd done. We ought to have been ladylike and lolled in the bed. Then at seven we should have sauntered down to the dining room and waited for whatever Mrs. O'Shay saw fit to serve up. But where we came from, everybody did his share.

Mrs. O'Shay wheeled back at us. "And what have you done to my kitchen?"

Lottie's shoulders squared. "We've cleaned it up," she said. "It was filthy."

The word hung in the room. Terrible wrath and something else burned in Mrs. O'Shay's small eyes. We'd found her out. She couldn't cook and wouldn't clean.

"Your aunt never complained," she said, low and mean.

Our aunt didn't dare. We held our ground, though I was scared. The spatula hung a little dangerously in Lottie's hand.

Mrs. O'Shay missed a moment, then turned back on Aunt Euterpe. "I was cook and housekeeper to poor old Mr. Fleischacker before you ever come on the scene, *Mrs.* Fleischacker. And how you nabbed him, I'll never know!"

I liked to have passed out. Where we came from, people didn't talk to you like that.

"Me and Bridget are done," Mrs. O'Shay snarled. "Let them ignorant country girls cook your meals and fetch and carry for you. You've seen the last of us! And you can have your house keys back."

She plunged a big red hand into her apron pocket.

Then the doggonedest thing happened. Mrs. O'Shay's face went a quick purple. Her mouth flew open, wide as Mammoth Cave. She cut loose with a scream they could have heard back in Ireland.

Little Bridget jumped away from her. Aunt Euterpe fell back. Mrs. O'Shay jerked her hand out of her pocket and held it up before her horrified face. Attached to her longest finger was a snapping turtle.

It wasn't as big as they get. It wasn't even as big as a saucer. But it was big enough to have a good strong bite to it. And it didn't turn loose, though Mrs. O'Shay flapped her hand and the turtle like a wild woman. Its shell swooped in the room with its tiny tail twitching behind.

Screaming like a banshee, Mrs. O'Shay danced a jig of pain across the kitchen. Then she was past us and out the back way, wringing her hand and the reptile as she went. Little Bridget followed at a safe distance, shedding her apron at the door.

In the yard Tip set to barking.

Then it was just Lottie and me over by the range. And Aunt Euterpe turned to stone in the doorway. Behind her Granddad's old voice welled up from the dining room. "Where's my breakfast, anyhow?"

Then Buster piped: "Anybody see my turtle?"

Even with a hearty breakfast in us, Lottie and I were cast in gloom and guilt. There were no two ways about it. We'd run off all Aunt Euterpe's household help.

She drooped dreadfully at her place, though she'd polished off her eggs. It seemed to be the worst morning of her life. "Good help is so hard to find nowadays," she sighed.

"It'd be the first good help you ever had." Granddad spoke around a mouthful of pancakes. There'd been no

conversation till now. Nobody had asked him about seeing the real Lillian Russell last night at the theater. And
he hadn't offered.

Aunt Euterpe folded and refolded a dingy napkin. "I
believe I had better move into a hotel. Quite respectable
people are now living in the better hotels."

Lottie and I verged on tears. "No, girls," Aunt Euterpe
said, "do not take it to heart. I was rattling around in this
big old house anyway. No one pays a call on me."

We'd come to that conclusion on our own. A silver
tray was out on her marble-topped hat stand. It was for
the visiting cards of ladies who might call on her. Nobody had.

"Ain't people neighborly a'tall?" Granddad asked.

"I am in a hard place without Mr. Fleischacker." Aunt
Euterpe fingered her brooch. "A widow's lot is not easy."
She clung to the grim little ornament at her throat.

"What's in that brooch anyway?" Granddad squinted
down the table over his specs. He saw better without
them.

"It is a lover's knot of human hair," Aunty said, "all I
have left of the person of Mr. Fleischacker."

"You snipped it off his head?" Granddad seemed interested. Buster certainly was.

"In a manner of speaking," Aunt Euterpe replied. "He
was bald as an egg, but I cut it out of his beard. After
he was in his coffin, of course."

Lottie set aside her fork.

Granddad pondered. The knot of hair under the dome of Aunty's brooch was gray.

"I take it he wasn't took from you in the prime of his life," Granddad said, not unkindly.

"He was eighty-four."

Granddad blinked. Whatever age he was, he wasn't yet eighty-four himself.

Aunt Euterpe sighed further, and I read Lottie's mind. She'd like to get Aunty out of those black widow's weeds she wore. And if it had been left up to Lottie, she'd have stuck that awful human-hair brooch in the stove.

"You see," Aunt Euterpe said, "I was Mr. Fleischacker's secretary. I sat in his outer office and handwrote his letters for him. That was before the advent of the typewriter. I wouldn't know how to operate a typewriter. . . ." She tapered off.

"Well, it was honest work," Granddad declared.

Aunt Euterpe turned over a hopeless hand. "Mr. Fleischacker was a widower. I was his secretary. When we wed, people talked."

"What about?" said Buster, again alert at the wrong moment.

We quieted Buster, and a stillness descended.

I suppose I saw then why Aunty had bothered to invite us to Chicago. She was lonely. I'd had to come to this city jammed with people to see a soul as lonely as hers. It stirred my heart. And Lottie's too.

Breakfast was over. There wasn't any pie. We sat in the airless room, hearing the tick of the landing clock. I only wished I could do something about Aunt Euterpe's sad situation. After all, we owed her something after running off her household help.

Doomishly she broke the silence. "Mr. Fleischacker's first wife's friends cut me dead. And we knew no one else." She stared away at an empty future through the spectacles that gripped her narrow nose.

A tapping sound came across the scrubbed kitchen floor, drawing nearer. Tip stuck his muzzle around the dining-room door. He'd worked the back door open and invited himself into the house. Aunt Euterpe seemed not to notice. Buster noticed, but sat still as a little soldier.

Hunkering, Tip skulked across the rug and disappeared under the table. We were country people. We never let animals into the house, not unless they were ready to cook and eat. But we were miles from our world. Tip seemed to settle somewhere near Buster's boots.

Aunt Euterpe's plight had Granddad baffled. His gnarled old hand worked his clenched chin. Lottie looked across at me. This was no problem for a man to solve.

At length Granddad drew himself up and boomed, "You need to get out more, Terpie. This house is a tomb. It's time we were off to the fair. These children need educating. They's green as—"

"Papa, I couldn't possibly—"

"Me and the boy will be lookin' over the heavy machinery and the farm implements. We may drop by the Pennsylvania pavilion to see if the Liberty Bell's still cracked. You can show these girls the womanly things, Terpie."

"The cars will be so crowded at this time of day," Aunt Euterpe sighed.

"Then have your man bring your carriage around," said Granddad.

Aunt Euterpe quaked. "Flanagan was out yesterday, Papa. He won't like—"

"You leave Flanagan to me," said Granddad in a final way.

Midmorning found us swaying along in Aunt Euterpe's closed carriage. Granddad and Buster rode on the box with Flanagan. We heard the low rumble of a conversation starting up. Aunt Euterpe had viewed Lottie and me with dismay when she saw us dressed again today in yesterday's finery. She wore a different set of widow's weeds and a hat like a heavily veiled coal scuttle.

As we rolled past number 1350 Lake Shore Drive, she pointed out once more the great palace of Mrs. Potter Palmer, the queen of Chicago society.

"There are no locks or knobs on her outer doors," Aunt Euterpe breathed. "A visitor is admitted only by servants forever posted just inside."

My land, I thought. Like jail.

"A visiting card left upon Mrs. Palmer passes through the gloved hands of twenty-seven servants and social secretaries before she sees it," said Aunt Euterpe wanly, ". . . if she sees it."

We turned at the water tower past the Farwells' pair of mansions, then on down Michigan Avenue, over the bridge, and by the new art institute and the skeleton of the Auditorium Hotel rising out of the ground. After a time we were on Prairie Avenue, and Aunt Euterpe could tell you who lived in every mansion: the Armours, the Fields, the Pullmans, Kimball the piano maker. She knew them all from her distance. And my, how she admired them.

We clipped along past their mighty gates in a traffic of fine carriages and charabancs and five-glass landaus, drawn by high-stepping chestnut trotters, many in silver-mounted harness. The horses' hooves were blackened like patent leather.

It seemed to comfort Aunt Euterpe to be in so fine a district. But then from above, Granddad and Flanagan, old friends now, burst into song to serenade the neighborhood:

Did ye ever hear tell of McGarry—
Mick McGarry? Comes from Derry?
When he got half tight, he was sparry—
Oh, he was such a divil to fight!

Sure he'd fall out wid soldier or sailor,
Or a nailer or a tailor;
Be jabers! He'd tackle a jailer.
He was dyin' to fight ev'ry night.

Aunt Euterpe sank back against the buttoned upholstery
and took refuge behind her veils. She huddled there like
she was coming away from Lincoln's funeral as onward
we rolled, heading for the fair.

THE WORST DAY IN AUNT EUTERPE'S LIFE

Part Two

U nder the summer sun the exposition glittered like a city carved from crystal. The flags of all nations snapped in the china-blue sky. The doorway of the Transportation Building was a solid-gold sunburst. A mass of roses bloomed across the islands with the Japanese temples. And over the domes and spires of the fair the captive balloon looked for the curve of the earth.

We left Granddad and Buster at the Hall of Electricity. There, it was said, over a long-distance telephone you could hear music being played in New York.

Aunt Euterpe had seemed to rally. She shooed Lottie and me into the Horticultural Hall to pay a quick call on the giant cactus in there. But she was in a rush to get us to the Woman's Building, which was to her the beating heart of the fair. After all, Mrs. Potter Palmer ruled the Board of Lady Managers.

The Woman's Building stood on the lip of the lagoon like a villa of ancient Pompeii blown up to gigantic size. The building itself had been designed by a young woman, Miss Hayden. It was fine, of course, by far the finest building we'd ever set foot in.

As quick as you came inside, you were in a vast hall like a cathedral. There on one wall was a tremendous mural by Mrs. MacMonnies. It depicted cavewomen of prehistoric times, seeming to discover fire.

"Bringing enlightenment to their menfolk," Aunt Euterpe murmured behind her veil.

"Learning how to cook so they'll never get out of the kitchen," spoke Lottie into my other ear.

The pictures on the far wall showed modern women. To understand them took more education than I had. The women danced and played lutes across one panel. I comprehended them. In another, I thought they were flying a kite. But Aunt Euterpe said they were in the Pursuit of Knowledge. In the center scene three women and a girl picked apples off a tree. I thought I grasped that. But Aunt Euterpe said they were gathering the Fruits of the Arts and Sciences.

These pictures had been painted by Miss Mary Cassatt. Aunt Euterpe said she was the finest artist alive, and a great friend of Mrs. Palmer's.

We roamed room after room. Aunt Euterpe trod more firmly in this world full of the achievements of women. I believe I did too. It showed what women could do. They could paint and explore and discover. We could.

We came upon an exhibition called "The Model Farm Kitchen," though could there ever be such a wonder as we beheld? The range was fired by gas, so you'd never have to gather another stick of kindling. Water ran hot and cold straight into the sink. Electric lights hung down. A machine washed your clothes for you and wrung them out. Lottie and I couldn't look at each other for fear of laughing out loud.

There on the wall of The Model Farm Kitchen was a verse I tried to learn by heart to repeat to Mama. It was called "The Hymn of the Farm Wife":

Let the mighty and great
Roil in splendor and state!
I envy them not, I declare it.
I eat my own lamb,
My own chicken and ham,
I shear my own sheep and I wear it.

I have gardens and bowers,
I have fruits, I have flowers,
The lark is my morning's charmer;
To no one I bow,
So here's to the plow!
Long life and content to the farmer.

But it didn't ring true to Lottie. She suspected a man poet had thought it up.

We drifted on and came to the auditorium just in time to hear Susan B. Anthony on the subject of women's suffrage. Aunt Euterpe pulled us inside, and we were glad enough to sink into the velvet seats even if it meant being lectured to.

Miss Anthony's favorite subject was giving the vote to women. It seemed a long shot to me. But she was an elderly lady, full of years and wisdom. She spoke at length, banging the pulpit, and Aunt Euterpe was rapt.

As we filed out, Aunty exclaimed, "If women voted, we would throw the rascals out. We would purify politics!"

"Will we get the vote?" Lottie wondered.

"Certainly not," Aunt Euterpe said. "The men wouldn't hear of it."

We narrowly escaped another lecture. It was Miss Frances Willard and the temperance shouters, calling for the prohibition of all hard liquor. They planned to pray the country dry.

But Lottie put her foot down. First the model kitchen we'd never have. Then votes we'd never get. Lottie wasn't ready to hear about pouring all the whiskey in the ditch, which nobody was going to do.

Besides, Aunt Euterpe admitted it was teatime, and we'd missed our noonday meal. She claimed the best people took their tea at the Turkish pavilion. We strolled in that direction.

Oh, it was nice inside Turkey—cool with all that tile work and a fountain splashing in the center. To our delight an orchestra played in the background—all the new songs we hadn't heard: "In the Gloaming" and "Where Is My Wandering Boy Tonight?" and "Seeing Nellie Home."

Ladies sat at small marble tables around the fountain. You never saw such hats. The elastic that held mine on cut into my chin. Aunt Euterpe cast veiled looks at our getups. A smudge had appeared from somewhere on my best gabardine skirt.

"Make note of their posture," Aunt Euterpe murmured. "Pay attention to the way they hold their teacups." They were grand ladies, no question about that. And their corsets were so binding, they had no choice but to sit as rigid as the cavalry on parade.

Men in turbans brought our tea: finger sandwiches tangled in parsley, little cakes like crescent moons. Nothing to stick to your ribs, but pretty on the plate. The teacups were gold-banded, and the brass teapot spout was the flaring hood of a cobra snake.

Aunty couldn't very well drink tea through her veil. She threw it back. And froze.

Her gloved hand reaching for the teapot clasped her black bosom. "Girls, the table across the fountain," she gasped. "Don't look now."

We looked at once. Three of the elegantest ladies you ever saw sat around a little table. Their hat brims all but

skimmed one another. Points of lace fell from their elbows. There were silk tassels on their reticules.

"Girls," Aunt Euterpe breathed. "That is Mrs. Potter
Palmer."

We stared, and we weren't the only ones. Everybody
in the Turkish pavilion knew she was there. I suppose
I thought she ought to be wearing a gold crown, as she
was the queen of Chicago. But then, I'd never calculated
to set eyes on her at all. She was speaking in tones so low
and cultured, you couldn't hear. Her friends leaned in
to catch every word. I took them to be her ladies-in-
waiting.

"Mrs. Charles Henrotin," Aunt Euterpe whispered.
"Mrs. William Borden."

Mrs. Palmer was certainly something to see, though
not a minute younger than Aunt Euterpe. The sun had
never seen her skin. It was as perfect as the pearls that
roped her neck. She looked to have an excellent set of
teeth.

"Only think, girls," Aunt Euterpe sighed. "She sleeps
in Louis the Sixteenth's bed."

My land, I thought—though of course he'd be dead.

"Her underwear and stockings," Aunt Euterpe said
barely aloud, "are catalogued for opera, carriage, and re-
ception, for morning and evening."

Aunt Euterpe couldn't touch a bite, though Lottie and
I ate everything but the pattern on the plate. It was food
and drink to Aunty just to breathe the same air as Mrs.

Potter Palmer. This was by far the high moment of her day, and I wished for her sake it could last.

They brought more hot water for our tea. The whole room was chained to their chairs, nobody leaving ahead of Mrs. Palmer.

At last her party rose. When they dipped to retrieve their reticules and their fair programs, their hats were circular flower beds. Mrs. Palmer led the way, regally, around the fountain.

And something terrible overcame me. Oh, I expect it had been coming on right along. I suppose it had been creeping up on me from the moment Mama had put me in long skirts to go to the fair. I reckon it had been stealing up on me from the time I realized how lonely Aunty was.

Still, I seemed to be some other girl entirely as I scraped back my chair on the screeching tile. This other girl I'd become was on her feet now. Lottie's hand came out for me and missed. Now I was in Mrs. Palmer's path, blocking her way.

I'd taken leave of my senses, though my blank mind noticed small things. The pearl dewdrops on the silk roses of Mrs. Palmer's hat, things like that. Her eyes were surprised as her gaze fell upon me.

"Pardon me for butting in, Mrs. Palmer," I heard myself say. By ill chance the orchestra was resting. My countrified voice rang through the room and bounced off the tile.

I drew back my smudged skirt and dropped her the

first curtsy of my life, and the last. "I only wanted to say what a grand city you have here."

You could hear a pin drop. The room held its breath. There at my elbow rigor mortis had set in on Aunty. Lottie was poised for another grab at me.

The two ladies flanking Mrs. Palmer viewed me with alarm. But she nodded in her cultivated way. To me and the listening room she replied, "How pleased I am to hear you say so. Some of the Spanish nobility we have received have not been so favorably impressed."

My mind whirled, but I was encouraged by her reply. Too encouraged. "Me and Lottie," I blundered on, "are up here visiting with our aunt, Mrs. Fleischacker, over behind you on Schiller Street."

I pointed Aunty out. She stared at nothing, framed in veils, despair written all over her. "I'd like to make you acquainted with her."

"Ah," Mrs. Palmer said carefully. Then disaster outright befell us.

As if from a puff of infernal smoke Granddad appeared. He was just suddenly there, elbowing Mrs. Palmer out of the way, swatting his old curly-brimmed Panama on his knee.

"There you'ens are!" he roared in the room. "Helacatoot, Terpie, I've lost Buster!"

When I can bear to think of us next, we were well away from the Turkish pavilion. The exposition spread around us, a vast anthill of people, a haystack where a needle named Buster would be hard to locate. Aunt Euterpe moved like a woman in a terrible trance. Though I'd meant well, I'd robbed her of her last hope. I thought that once we found Buster, I'd offer to have myself arrested and put away someplace where I could do no more harm.

"Think, Granddad." Lottie gave his arm a good shake. "Where did you last see him?" We were hurrying now, though where, we didn't know.

"After we left the Electrical Hall, I took him over to the California pavilion to see the horse and rider made out of prunes," Granddad recalled. "Then we skated past the United States Government Building to view the weapons of destruction. After that I stood him a good meal at the German place we was at last night."

It wouldn't have taken Granddad long to get back to the Midway. We headed there now. "Then what?" Lottie said. "Think, Granddad."

"Well, I dropped in to see Little Egypt do her dance, and the boy went for a camel ride," Granddad admitted, stumping along. "I told him to meet me out front, but the little squirt didn't." Granddad was worried. Lottie and I were too, though we understood that Buster was quicksilver, there and gone before you knew.

The Midway was as crowded as before. Long lines waited to pay their fifty-cent pieces and ride the great wheel. The captive balloon had worked free of its moorings and vanished, but people were examining the cable. We stopped to inquire if Buster might have been riding the balloon when it drifted off to oblivion. But we were assured he hadn't been.

Small boys darted everywhere, none of them Buster. We made our way to A Street in Cairo, then saw we'd have to go door-to-door from one attraction to the next.

Aunt Euterpe followed, wordless. If she'd been herself, she'd have objected to going into anyplace with unruly crowds or half-dressed women. But she wasn't herself and never would be again, thanks to me.

Not all of the Midway attractions were gaudy. Hard by A Street in Cairo next door to the Laplanders' Village was a small, plain brick building. It was Professor Muybridge's Zoöpraxographical Hall.

Though unpromising, it wouldn't take long to search. It was only a single room like a laboratory with a fence across one side that the public could hang over. Over that fence we found Buster, hanging on Professor Muybridge's every word.

Granddad was well-nigh overcome with relief, but naturally wouldn't let on. He merely turned his attention to the professor, who was lecturing at the front of the room. He was old as the hills, with a long white beard like Father Time.

The professor had invented a way of placing photographs together on a clear strip. He put these pictures into a machine called a zoögyroscope that threw their images up on a blank wall. The pictures seemed to move. Horses appeared to race. The folds of skin on a hog's back rippled. Galloping tintypes, I thought. Seeing pictures come alive and race across a wall made me dizzy. Though they didn't race for long.

"Can you make 'em talk too?" called out Granddad. I believe this was mostly to let Buster know he'd been found.

"Well, sir," Professor Muybridge replied, "I have spoken to Mr. Edison about it. He undertakes to match sound on a phonograph to the movements of my pictures. But there is no way of amplifying it for a large gathering."

"Just a fad," Granddad decided, collecting Buster off the fence.

At the beer garden nearby the Bedouin Encampment, we discovered Flanagan, a little the worse for wear. He took us home. Granddad and Buster again rode shotgun for him up on the box.

That left us women in the cab of the carriage, and I was sick with shame. Waves of it washed over me.

"What in Sam Hill could you have been *thinking*?" Lottie barked in the consoling way of a sister.

"I just thought if I introduced Mrs. Palmer to Aunty, she might leave a card on her," I said in the mousiest voice I owned. "I just thought . . ."

"Never mind, child," Aunt Euterpe said. A black-gloved hand came out to me. "You meant well and knew no better. But all is lost. I think I had best go to live in a hotel in some other city."

We'd begun the day by running off Aunt Euterpe's household help. I'd ended it by running her out of town. Oh, how I wanted to light out for home right then, and never leave again. I wasn't ready for the world, and I couldn't figure out how it worked.

I draw a veil over the evening that followed. But then even this endless day came to its close. Lottie and I were in the bed when a tremendous rainstorm whipped up off the lake. Rain pounded the window. Lightning cracked. Thunder clapped.

Finally Lottie began to snort and then to giggle in the dark. Then by and by so did I. They say that once a turtle bites, he won't turn loose till it thunders. We were thinking what a relief it must be to Mrs. O'Shay, wherever she was.

Then we slept, trying not to imagine what tomorrow might hold in store.

POST CARD

THIS SIDE FOR CORRESPONDENCE

THE ADDRESS TO BE WRITTEN ON THIS SIDE

1¢ U.S. POSTAGE

Dear Mama and Dad,
This is the Women's
Building, Aunt Euterpe's
favorite attraction at
the fair. Tea followed.
  Y.L.P.,
     Rosie

Mr. and Mrs.
    Gideon Beckett
Rural Christian
         County

Illinois

THE GREATEST DAY IN GRANDDAD'S LIFE

Part One

It was to be Granddad's day from start to finish. He let us know this by turning up at the breakfast table with the tips of his moustache waxed sharp as spurs. His necktie was a new one to us, and may have been batiste. He'd buttoned a winged collar to his shirt.

More wondrous still, Buster at his elbow wore the dreaded artistic cravat under his Eton collar. He had an unnaturally scrubbed look. His hair stood out as if somebody had held him under the pump. In passing, Lottie dipped down for a look at Buster's ears and found them clean as whistles.

Lottie and I were back and forth from dining room

to kitchen, since we were all the household help Aunt Euterpe had. There was a pie in the oven. We'd found a sealed jar of pie cherries Lottie thought wouldn't poison us. The kitchen was our territory now. Come to find out, the butcher's boy and the grocer's boy would deliver at the back door. You didn't even have to lay in your own supplies. We marveled at what an easy job Mrs. O'Shay had given up.

When we were all at the breakfast table, Aunt Euterpe sat propped at her place in another of her shrouds. A string of black jet hung around her drawn neck. She had the look of a woman shorn of all hope, but she was there. A lesser woman would have taken to her bed after what we'd done to her.

"We'll have Flanagan take us down to the Congress Street station this morning," Granddad announced. He seemed to know Chicago like the back of his hand now. "We'll try out that new Alley Elevated train."

Though her life was over anyway, Aunt Euterpe quaked with alarm. It seemed that Chicago had built a railroad line with tracks laid high on stilts above the alleys. It was another way to get to the fair.

"It is thought to be unsafe," Aunt Euterpe said. "I don't mind for myself, but what would Adelaide say if these children . . ."

Aunt Euterpe fell silent before she conjured up a picture of Lottie and Buster and me squashed like june bugs when the elevated train jumped its tracks.

"It's progress," Granddad said, the last word on the subject.

To our surprise Aunty perked up some. "Papa, if we are going that near State Street, I'll take these girls to Marshall Field's store on the way. They need more clothes."

"Aunty," Lottie said, "we can't let you—"

"It is only money," Aunt Euterpe muttered, a bleak reminder that we'd robbed her of everything else.

Then Lottie saw her chance. "It is very good of you to be so generous, Aunty, especially in the circumstances. Rosie and I will make you a deal, fair and square."

A little curiosity crept into Aunt Euterpe's tired eyes. She seemed not to have slept a wink all night.

"We'll accept a gift of new outfits if you will get a new outfit for yourself. And not black, Aunty. Black is not right for your coloring, and you have mourned enough."

"Amen to that," Granddad put in from the other end of the table.

Aunty gazed down her own blackness. Now we weren't even going to let her dress the way she wanted to.

"Our shopping won't take long," said Lottie firmly. I suppose she pictured Marshall Field's store to be the size of the dry goods back home. "Then we can go on to the fair."

"We're not going to the fair!" Buster sang out suddenly. It made us jump. We'd begun to think he was too scrubbed to speak.

"Then where are we going?" said Lottie.

Now Buster and Granddad were grinning and elbowing each other, acting as foolish as the male sex so often
does.

"We're goin' to witness a spectacle that puts the fair to
shame!" Granddad crowed. Buster was riding his chair
like a half-broke pony. "Tell 'em, boy."

Buster blurted, "We've got us tickets to see Buffalo
Bill's Wild West and Congress of Rough Riders of the
World!"

We women received this news without comment, until Aunt Euterpe sighed, "Oh dear, cowboys and Indians.
Think how dusty it will be."

"And we're takin' Tip with us," Granddad declared. "If
I leave him behind—"

"He pines and gets off his feed," Lottie and I chanted
under our breath.

From beneath the table Tip heard his name men-
tioned. His tail thumped the floor.

Buffalo Bill had brought his Wild West and Congress
of Rough Riders show home from three years of enter-
taining the crowned heads of Europe. The Alley Elevated
built a station at Sixty-third Street expressly for people
flocking to this spectacle. It stood on fifteen acres opposite the fairgrounds themselves. Some people traveled to
Chicago and saw Buffalo Bill's show, then went home
again thinking they'd seen the Columbian Exposition.

You could understand why. The very coliseum we sat

in held eighteen-thousand people and seemed bigger than Chicago itself. We sat jammed onto a bleacher above the great artificial prairie where they promised us an authentic buffalo hunt and a reenactment of Custer's Last Stand.

Buster and Granddad waited restless for the gunplay and mayhem to begin. Between them sat Tip, who didn't mind where he was, as long as he got to go. We women sat behind in fresh finery. It seemed the outfits we'd brought from home were last year's fashions in Chicago.

I was newly turned out in a middy blouse over a white pleated skirt that swept to my shoes. My new hat carried out the marine theme with streamers down the back. Lottie looked all grown up with ruffles high on her neck and a wreath of silken lilies of the valley around the crown of her hat. We both had reticules now, and lacy handkerchiefs thrust into our belts.

Between us Aunt Euterpe was all in dove gray. A hint of shell pink showed in one of the flowers on her un-veiled hat. Her face was still in mourning, but the rest of her was much relieved. Lottie was right. Black hadn't suited her coloring. She was improved, but not used to it yet.

I see us still amid that multitude, there in the filtered afternoon light, the air heavy-scented with lemonade and horse. Now Mr. William Sweeny's Cowboy Band is strik-ing up the overture, a medley of "Tenting Tonight on the Old Campground" and "Hello, Central, Give Me Heaven."

And now Buster's piping up. "Granddad, why do they call him Buffalo Bill?"

"He shot buffalo for the Kansas Pacific Railroad in his early days," Granddad explained loud enough to inform everyone around us. "He had his own style of stampedin' the critters into a circle. He shot the back ones to keep their leaders circlin'. It was like shooting ducks in a ditch."

"Was he kill-crazy, Granddad?"

Granddad reared back. "He was killin' meat to feed the workers buildin' the railroad, boy. We killed to eat in them days."

Then Granddad burst into verse, as he was apt to do:

Buffalo Bill, Buffalo Bill
Never missed and never will;
Always aims and shoots to kill,
And the company pays his buffalo bill.

Lottie sighed. "The next thing Granddad's going to claim," she predicted, "is that he knew Colonel Cody personally."

Aunt Euterpe moaned.

"Oh, yes," Granddad expanded, standing now to address our general vicinity, "the noble buffalo was the

Marshall Field's store of the great plains. The meat was food. The dressed hides was moccasins and robes. The hair was twisted into ropes. Green hides made pots for cookin' over buffalo-chip fires. The small bones made needles, and the ribs was dog-sled runners. The hooves melted down for glue. And from the horns come spoons and various utensils. Yessir," said Granddad to our neighbors, "the buffalo come in handy."

The band struck up "The Star-Spangled Banner," and we were all upstanding, then rustling our programs.

The show opened with a Grand Review of the mounted troops of the world's great armies: the United States, France, Germany, the British Empire, and Russia. They wore the finest uniforms you ever saw, dimly seen through the dust they raised.

Then on came Miss Annie Oakley, a dead shot. She could knock anything down from a galloping horse. She even fired backward over her shoulder while looking in a hand mirror. Aunt Euterpe looked in her own lap because of the shortness of Miss Oakley's buckskin skirt.

Yokes of oxen drew emigrant trains of covered wagons across the prairie and we were assured they were the exact wagons in actual use thirty-five years before. The air was thick now, but there was hardly time to breathe. Cowboys roped wild ponies and bucked on broncos. Mexicans demonstrated the lasso. Kaiser Wilhelm's Postdamer Reds led a cavalry charge, and so did the Prince of

Wales's Twelfth Lancers. Then a grand tableau of the Sioux people, in the field and out on the path. Buster was on his feet the whole time.

The crowd was noisier than the band as the excitement mounted. The last event before the intermission would feature the actual Deadwood Mail Coach. It was to be attacked by Indians and rescued by Buffalo Bill in person. There were ants in Granddad's pants now, and Tip was up in a crouch.

To add interest, dignitaries and famous celebrities were invited to ride in the Deadwood coach as players in this drama. Out from under the bleachers rattled the stagecoach, drawn by six stampeding steeds. As it circled the track, the audience sent around a wave of ovation. Tipping their silk hats from within the coach were Mr. Altgeld, the governor of Illinois, and Carter H. Harrison, the mayor of Chicago. Aunt Euterpe stirred some at the sight of such socially prominent men.

On the coach's second turn it was being chased by an Indian war party riding bareback on spotted ponies. Some in the audience shied at their war cries and paint. But Buster was practically standing on Granddad's head. Though the driver cracked his whip like anything, the war party drew ever nearer, waving ornamental axes. Now the governor and mayor were hanging on inside.

With a burst of music from the Cowboy Band, Buffalo Bill himself pounded onto the field astride a burnished mount. Behind him galloped his Rough Riders, their hat brims turned back, their bandannas back to front around their necks, their chaps fleecy.

The afternoon sun fell like a spotlight on Buffalo Bill in a hat white as swansdown. His fringed buckskin coat fit like a glove. His breeches looked painted on. His silver-toed boots were the tanned hides of animals too rare to have names. He leaned into the wind, and his waxed moustaches flowed against his face. Though he'd left his slender days behind him, he was the finest-looking man I ever saw.

He and his Rough Riders pursued the war party at a stately pace, receiving an ovation. After all, Buffalo Bill was the most famous man alive.

As they passed our way another time, the Indians' ponies were even with the rear wheels of the Deadwood coach. Some of the party, bristling with feathers, were fixing to leap onto the coach roof. Buffalo Bill's Rough Riders were closing from behind. It was a thrilling moment. And it was too much for Tip.

He sprang from the bleacher. There was a sudden space between Granddad and Buster. Tip soared almost over the heads of the people in front of us. He lit running. Nobody had ever seen him move this fast, not even at dinner time. He was gone like greased lightning. Now he streaked onto the field, his ears laid back, his tongue lolling out. The Indian ponies swerved as Tip shot after the coach itself.

I suppose he thought it was going to town, and he didn't want to be left behind.

The crowd gave him a round of applause. Some of them may have thought Tip was part of the show. Coach, war party, Buffalo Bill, and his Rough Riders had thundered past us. There was nothing to see but a cloud of dust.

"Hecka-tee," Granddad said. Buster was speechless.

It occurred to me that Tip might be gone for good. Who that would kill quicker, Granddad or Buster, I didn't like to think. We sat there stunned. Aunt Euterpe seemed as bewildered as she often was in our company.

Then around the course they came once more, the Rough Riders dispersing the war party, who fanned out in retreat. Firing magnificent silver six-shooters at the sky, Buffalo Bill drew nigh the team and brought coach and horses to a whirlwind halt. His own mount reared beautifully.

Three heads appeared at a window of the Deadwood coach: the governor, the mayor, and Tip. Somehow they'd let him inside, so he was in at the grand finale. Again the crowd roared. Tip barked.

Granddad creaked to his feet. He parted the people ahead of us with his stick, making his way down onto the field. The band played "The Cowboy March" to signal intermission.

But all eyes were on Granddad. There was still some

glow to his ice-cream suit. His curly-brimmed Panama rode firm on his head. He waved his stick. "Come on, Tip! Leave them gentlemen be and come on down from there!"

I saw it all. I wouldn't have blinked. Buffalo Bill turned his horse. The perfectly trained beast took a prancing step or two nearer Granddad. Buffalo Bill leaned down from the saddle.

"Si?" Buffalo Bill called out. "Well, blame my skeets if it isn't Silas Fuller!"

Granddad threw back his head and looked at the magnificence of Colonel Cody. "Hello there, Bill," he said. "How's business?"

"It is you, isn't it, Si? You old owlhoot." Buffalo Bill sat back in his saddle and tipped up his hat.

Yes, it was. It was Silas Fuller, our granddad. Aunt Euterpe was a statue beside me. Lottie's jaw dropped.

"How long has it been, Si?" Buffalo Bill wanted to know. Both he and Granddad were full-voiced men.

"Twenty-nine years since the Battle of Tupelo," said Granddad, "give or take."

"Did you ever make better than corporal?" Buffalo Bill was asking, and I nudged Aunt Euterpe.

"Was Granddad in the Civil War?" We'd seen no medals.

"He couldn't wait to get into the fight," she said. "He left a wife and two young daughters behind. My mother never drew an easy breath till the end of the war."

"Afraid Granddad wouldn't come back," I said.

"No," said Aunty. "Afraid he would."

Down on the field Buffalo Bill was saying to Granddad, "Dog my cats, Si! I might have known you'd turn up again like a bad penny. You always were everywhere at once."

"That's me," Granddad croaked, "the bride at every wedding and the corpse at every funeral. Say, listen, Bill, let me collect Tip. Then I'd like you to meet my family."

Behind her gloved hand Aunt Euterpe shrieked.

THE GREATEST DAY IN GRANDDAD'S LIFE

Part Two

T hough it was intermission, few on our side of the coliseum budged from their bleachers. Their eyes were trained on the governor of the state and the mayor of the city easing themselves down from the Deadwood coach. The crowd may have wondered who the old owlhoot Colonel William F. Cody was talking to happened to be. A rumor circulated near us that Granddad was Mr. Mark Twain. Which he wouldn't have minded.

Granddad waved us down and we had to go, though Aunt Euterpe hung back. Buster moved in a dream, drawing nearer every boy's idol, Buffalo Bill.

"Here they are now," said Granddad. "Bill, I'd like to make you acquainted with my daughter. Terpie, this here is Bill Cody."

Aunty faltered on uneven ground. Colonel Cody swept off his hat in the most graceful gesture I was ever to see a man make. His hair fell to his broad buckskinned shoulders. Aunty put forth a trembling hand and the colonel took it. He bent and his moustaches grazed her gloved wrist.

She swayed like a poplar, and I thought she might pass from us. The most famous of American men had just kissed her wrist in the presence of the governor of the state and the mayor of the city, with an audience of thousands behind her. "Ma'am," Colonel Cody said, "you bring a beautiful dignity to the proceedings."

The cat had her tongue.

"And I take it that these lovely young ladies are your daughters?"

This shook her loose. "Oh, no." She turned a startled gaze upon us. "They're Adelaide's girls—my nieces."

The colonel liked to blind me. His shirtfront was gold lace. The studs were diamonds big as filberts. When he took my hand, I turned giddy. He passed along to Lottie, who went weak in the knee but held her ground.

Now it was Buster's turn. "Boy, tell him who you are," said Granddad, who was forever forgetting our names.

Buster was only as high as the colonel's belt buckle, which was encrusted with turquoises. He was apt to hang his head in new company. But he gazed up now in a somewhat sanctified way. To our astonishment he said, "LeRoy Beckett, sir. At your service."

He *was* LeRoy Beckett, of course. But the fact that LeRoy was his real first name was his darkest secret. Now I suppose he thought Buster was a name too young and undignified.

The colonel reached into his breast pocket. "Well, LeRoy, I believe this belongs to you."

He held out a silver dollar plugged neatly through the center. Whether Colonel Cody had himself used it for target practice or not, he didn't say. He only pressed it into Buster's hand. That silver dollar rode in Buster's pocket forever after.

The governor and the mayor were in no hurry to go. True politicians, they relished the colonel's company before this big audience of voters. "John Altgeld," said the governor, extending a hand to Granddad.

"Si Fuller from down in Christian County," Granddad replied. "I'll shake your hand, though I'm a Republican from the day we put the Railsplitter into office." Granddad reached a glad hand past him to Mayor Carter Harrison. "Mayor, I'd like to make you acquainted with my daughter Miz Fleischacker, from up on Schiller Street. Terpie, here's His Honor."

Aunty lurched in that way she had. But the mayor was

as smooth as his silk hat. Doffing it, he said, "Would that be August Fleischacker's—"

"Wife," Aunty murmured, her face coloring like sunset. "The second one. I have been in widow's weeds until very lately. This morning, in fact." She fell into a confused silence.

"Your late husband, ma'am, was a valued member of our business community," said the mayor. "Before The Fire, of course."

"So good of you to say so," said Aunty in a voice faint and far-off.

This was our moment in the sun. I was bound and determined to remember it always, and so I have. But the Cowboy Band was playing "She's Only a Bird in a Gilded Cage," and the intermission was all but over.

When Colonel Cody learned that we ladies had been in bleacher seats, he said he wouldn't stand for it. The bleachers would do for Granddad and Buster and Tip. But we were to watch the rest of the show from the colonel's own box. Evidently it was reserved for fashionable ladies and crowned heads if they were in town.

The colonel snapped his fingers. An usher appeared out of thin air to show us the way to our box seats. The governor and mayor withdrew, in search of voters.

"Aunty," I said as we went, "maybe now that you know the mayor—"

"No, child," she said. "In the social world it is not the

men who matter." But she was flushed from her moment
of fame.

The colonel's box offered front-row seats thrust out a little onto the field itself. It was draped in red, white, and
blue bunting caught up with silver horseshoes. The usher
opened a low door, and we were swept inside as the band
opposite us struck up "After the Ball."

A row of little gold chairs with plush seats filled the
box. At the far end a lady sat. She had a good full figure,
putting me in mind of Mama, or Lottie. Though *this* figure was encased in the finest white lace you ever saw. I
cannot speak for her feet, as her skirts were long and
sweeping. Her delicate white-gloved hand rested atop the
knob of a closed parasol. We couldn't see her face for her
hat.

I have to go on about that hat. I never saw its equal
before or since. It was of the finest straw, white. The
swooping brim must have been three feet across. It
dipped down over one shoulder, and the crown on it was
as big as a chimney. An enormous watered-silk black bow
was held in place by a diamond brooch. We stood trans-
fixed. She turned in the gracefullest gesture toward us,
and we saw her face.

Lottie caught her breath, and the tears started in my
eyes. Aunty faltered. She was the most beautiful woman
we'd ever laid eyes on. Her pale blond hair was dressed up
against the sweep of her hat. Her complexion was perfec-

tion. Where Mrs. Potter Palmer wore ropes of pearls, this lady's swan neck was encircled with diamonds. I wondered if there was a crowned head under that hat.

She smiled slightly and nodded nearly in our direction. But I had learned a hard lesson. Out here in the world, you thought twice before speaking to anybody you weren't introduced to. Besides, my tongue was tied by her beauty. There was a scent of tuberoses in the box, and it must have come from her.

We bumbled into our seats, keeping some distance. The second act of the show burst upon us. It was the buffalo hunt.

Rolling eyes and throwing clods, the herd thundered back and forth before us. Rounding them up with many a fancy maneuver was Buffalo Bill, now changed into another outfit. To back him up were all the champion horsemen of the Sioux nation: Kicking Bear and No Neck and Jack Red Cloud. They were all over the place.

From the corner of my eye I observed the lady. She didn't slump against the chair back. She sat forward, and it showed the lovely line of her back. She was corseted tight as a tick. I saw how painful that much beauty must be.

At long last they got all those buffalos corralled and herded off. The band broke into "Buffalo Gals, Won't You Come Out Tonight?" The lady turned our way a little shyly. Of course we were strangers to her. Then we heard her voice, like music. "Isn't it awfully dusty?" she remarked.

Without thinking, Aunt Euterpe replied, "I said it would be."

"Are you enjoying the show?" the lady asked me.

"Right much," I heard myself answer, "though I expect my brother Buster and Granddad like it better."

"Yes, and your dog seems to be interested in a career in show business." She smiled.

Come to think of it, it was thanks to Tip that we were sitting in this box talking to this lady. "Well, he isn't good for anything else," I said, "excepting to keep Granddad company."

"Your grandfather and Colonel Cody are old friends?" The lady just touched her throat with a gloved hand. She wore a ring with a large stone over the glove. I'd never seen that before. There was so much I'd never seen.

Aunt Euterpe leaned around me to reply. "Oh, yes, Papa and the colonel were in the war together." She was more and more at ease in this lady's company.

The lady nodded. "Old comrades-in-arms," she said, like more music. "And yet men at their most warlike are less cruel than women."

Aunt Euterpe started. "I couldn't agree with you more," she replied, no doubt thinking of all those ladies who'd never left a card on her. The flowers on her hat quivered and the next act began.

It was Colonel Cody again in still another costume, presenting "Unique Feats of Sharpshooting" on and off his horse. He was not a young man anymore. The rumor was that he fired buckshot so he was bound to hit something. But as Granddad would very likely say, it was all show business anyway.

We came then to the grand finale with every member of the cast, man, woman, and child, on horse or afoot. The field became the Black Hills of Dakota. We were to have the Battle of the Little Big Horn and the last charge of General Custer.

For a duel to the death, it had many a diversion. Buck Taylor, the King of the Cowboys, rode on his horse and under it. Utah Frank showed off a good deal of rope work. Colonel Cody led charge after charge, and the Germans and the Russians got into it.

But at last, somebody being General George Armstrong Custer made his last stand, took a bullet, and toppled off his horse. Somebody impersonating the late Chief Sitting Bull won the day.

A musical interlude followed to let the dead get up from where they fell and leave the field. Then the whole cast came back, the two-legged and the four-legged, to take their bows. The Rough Riders of all nations held high their flags and totems as the band played "Over the Waves" and "The Columbian March."

Then out rode Colonel William F. Cody for one last time, miraculously changed into an all-white outfit heavily embroidered. His horse pawed the air, and he raised his hat as the audience gave him one last standing ovation.

It was over, but the colonel urged his horse straight at

our box. He drew up and handed across the bunting a spray of sweet-smelling carnations in the colors of the American flag. They were for Aunt Euterpe.

"Oh, no!" she cried out. "Never in my life . . ." But she clutched those flowers to her. It did my heart good. What I wouldn't have given for Mama to see it, and to be handed flowers herself.

Then in Buffalo Bill's hand was, somehow, a nosegay of violets tied up in a silver ribbon. He was offering it to me, and another like it for Lottie. I remember yet his great gauntleted hand offering posies to those two country girls we were.

Without prompting, the vast white horse moved on. Now Colonel Cody sat there in the sky, above the beautiful lady. She looked up at him with her modest smile, and the audience craned to see her. From nowhere at all the colonel flourished a great spray of American Beauty roses and handed them over. She received them like a princess of the realm.

In a voice of sounding brass, he called out to the coliseum, "Ladies, Gentlemen, Children, I give you the toast of America—Miss Lillian Russell!"

Behind her glove Aunt Euterpe gave another of her shrieks.

The band struck up again "After the Ball," the song made famous by Lillian Russell, and the crowd went crazy, singing along: "After the ball is over, after the break of day . . ."

She set aside her parasol and stood, turning in a
sweeping way to greet her public. She dropped a curtsy
that would have graced any European court. And I read
Lottie's mind. This fallen woman who painted her face
and had had three husbands and was barred from the
Washington Park clubhouse was everything that Lottie
would like to be. And I felt the same.

Between us Aunt Euterpe sagged.

You wouldn't believe how fast Granddad made it to
our box once he'd heard Miss Lillian Russell was in it. He
was way ahead of Buster. He was way ahead of Tip. His
specs were at the end of his nose and his new necktie was
askew, and he was very nearly winded.

Cradling her roses, Miss Russell put out her hand to
him. "And you are Granddad, I believe?"

His gnarled old mitt came out to trap her gloved
fingertips. "Ma'am, I'm crude as a ripsawed plank," he
croaked, "but you have no greater admirer in the state of
Illinois."

This was a pretty speech in its way, but Lottie and I
worried about what might come next. Then it came.

"Are you acquainted with my daughter Miz Fleischacker?" Granddad asked. "She don't get out much,
but here she is."

"Ah," Miss Russell said uncertainly, drawing back a
little.

Then, without hardly wavering at all, Aunt Euterpe
rose to this unexpected occasion. She spoke firmly. "Miss

Russell," she said, "you do our city an honor with your presence."

Now Miss Russell's hand came out to meet Aunty's. "I will remember your kind words, Mrs. Fleischacker, when I have forgotten the snubs of others in the society of Chicago."

And Lottie and I saw how things could be between two ladies of real refinement, even if Society wouldn't know them.

Tip sailed into our midst then. He had to be talked out of jumping on Miss Russell's skirts. And after Tip came Buster.

"Boy, come and meet the greatest lady of the American stage." Granddad grabbed for him. "Ma'am," he said, "this here's my grandson, Bus—LeRoy. Boy, this here is Miss Lillian Russell!"

Buster beheld her, this perfect woman in her unforgettable hat, with her armload of roses, her lovely smile.

"Did they name you for our horse?" Buster inquired.

CHICAGO HISTORICAL SOCIETY

Dear Mama and Dad,
We went to Buffalo Bill's
Wild West Show this
afternoon. Granddad
and Buster's favorite
attraction. Tip's too.
    Then we met Miss
Lillian Russell in the
flesh (the real one,
a lady).
                Y.L.D.,
                Rosie

Mr. and Mrs.
    Gideon Beckett
Rural Christian
                County
    Illinois

6 PM
1893

An Invitation
for Aunt Euterpe

O ur days at the great exposition began to flicker past us. We came home weary that day, and footsore the day after that. Now we were picking the fair clean. We visited the pavilions of all nations. And when we'd worked through them, we called on all the state pavilions and the one for the territories of Arizona, Oklahoma, and New Mexico.

We fed off the free samples at Agricultural Hall. And we had us ground beef patties on buns they were calling "hamburgers." Granddad and Buster climbed over every locomotive in the Transportation Building and examined every fish in the Fisheries Building. Aunt Euterpe marched Lottie and me past every last picture in the Palace of Fine

Arts. She was as good as her word about showing us all the fair might have to teach us. But then, I supposed she saw that her own Chicago days were numbered.

One afternoon we returned by steamboat, sailing from the exposition pier, bound for Van Buren Street. We stood on the deck, feeling the breeze in our faces and the slap of the waves on the bow. The great city on the curve of the lake stood tall between us and the setting sun. Surely I must have wondered how we could go home again after all we'd seen.

That was the day we found the envelope on the front hall floor when we got back to Schiller Street. Starting, Aunt Euterpe swept it up before Tip could get at it. She tore it open while we were still jostling in around her, and held up a visiting card.

There, I thought. Now she has a card for her silver tray. She read it out: MRS. DANFORTH EVANS

Behind me Lottie caught her breath, then fell silent.

"Mercy," Aunty murmured, "she is the wife of a dean at the University of Chicago . . . very distinguished . . . an excellent family . . . I do not know her . . ."

Aunty sidestepped into her front parlor for some privacy. We followed. She pulled a larger card out of the envelope and settled her spectacles to read it.

It was an invitation. Mr. and Mrs. Danforth Evans requested the pleasure of Aunty's company at home on South Michigan Avenue for a musical evening, dancing with supper to follow.

Aunty looked up, bewildered. "But I am in mourning."

"No you ain't," Granddad said.

She read on, her eyes bugging. The invitation was to include Miss Lottie and Miss Rosie Beckett, Mr. Silas Fuller, and Master Buster Beckett.

She looked up bemused at the bunch of us around her. What a peaceful life she'd led before we came. Now were we the cause of this sudden invitation too? Or was being seen in the company of the mayor and the governor somehow behind it? Granddad himself looked stumped and unusually innocent. For once, though, I was blameless and in the clear, as far as I could figure.

"Papa," Aunty said in desperation, "I see no reason why you and the boy should accept—"

"Wouldn't miss it!" Granddad crowed. "It will give this boy a chance to see how polite society conducts theirselves. It might knock a rough edge or two off him." He thumped Buster lightly. He was still cranky about Buster asking Miss Russell if she'd been named after our horse.

Aunty fetched up a sigh like a sob. And Lottie said, "When?" Only that.

Looking again at the invitation, Aunt Euterpe shrieked. "My stars! Tomorrow night. How sudden! What can it— girls, you have nothing to wear. *I* have nothing to wear!"

She turned on Granddad. "Flanagan will have to take us. It is an excellent neighborhood, very select. Home to the Seips, Yerkes the streetcar magnate, the R. T. Cranes. Only the sifted few. Papa, you will be responsible for making sure Flanagan is clean-shaven."

We'd never seen Aunty so animated. She was truly out of mourning now, and nearly out of breath.

Upstairs, when we were skinning off our fair clothes, I watched Lottie like a hawk. She knew more about this turn of events than she was letting on.

Last week I'd have plagued her till she told me. But now I'd been to the fair. I'd been made acquainted with Colonel William F. Cody, and I was in long skirts. True, I'd stumbled and fallen over Mrs. Potter Palmer. But I was more of a woman now. I was not yet a woman of the world, but I had a toe in the door. I didn't deign to quiz Lottie. Besides, I'd be fourteen in the fall.

Lottie was acting peculiar, jerking the pins out of her hat and looking around distracted. She flopped on the bed with one shoe on and one shoe off. She was about beside herself, but I said nothing. I bided my time.

There was to be no exposition for us women that next day. Granddad and Buster were off early to see Gentleman James J. Corbett, the heavyweight champion of the world. He was demonstrating the use of the punching bag at a gymnasium on the Midway.

Aunt Euterpe and Lottie and I spent the day turning State Street upside down for outfits suitable to a musical evening, dancing with supper to follow. A strange and unknown fate was about to hurl us into polite society, and we had to look the part.

Worse, we'd have to buy straight off the rack and hope for the best. I leaned to pink, but Lottie said my hair would kill it. I leaned to seafoam green, but she said every red-headed girl in North America leaned to green. Aunty would have fallen back on black for herself, but Lottie and I wouldn't have it. We were all near the end of our patience when she conducted us off to lunch at the Siegel Cooper store.

Then she watched every move of our table manners and made comments.

It was as hard a day as I ever put in. Give me the butter and egg business every time. But the money poured off Aunt Euterpe like Niagara Falls. By the afternoon we were all outfitted from the skin onward. That included stiff muslin underdrawers and two petticoats apiece. "I know they are not comfortable," Aunt Euterpe said. "They are not meant to be comfortable."

We were invited for half past eight. Aunty said that's when we would leave Schiller Street, to keep from getting there too early.

Lottie and I were down in the front hall first, fussing over each other. I never was able to do much about my hair. But Lottie had got it up off my neck, and that made me feel grown-up enough to go.

I was in ivory satin with a ribbon run round the neck. Lottie was in lavender, which brought out her eyes. Even in the hard glare of gas flame she glowed with a beauty she would always keep. We neither of us wore jewelry. We didn't have any to wear. But Lottie said too much jewelry was unsuitable for girls of our years.

Aunt Euterpe came down the stairs, almost handsome in points of brown lace. We'd warned her against her human-hair brooch. At her waist she wore the last of Colonel Cody's carnations.

Granddad and Buster came down the stairs sparring with each other after having watched Gentleman Jim Corbett. To our relief Granddad wore his second-best, the black alpaca with the baggy knees. He'd brought back the winged collar to go with it. A bow tie clung to his bristly old Adam's apple like a black moth. Buster was once again in good order with his socks up and his cravat on. But he looked dubious.

The Danforth Evans residence was nowhere near as grand as Mrs. Potter Palmer's castle. But it was fine in its way. It backed on Lake Michigan, and the front porch was wide and welcoming. Music drifted from its bright windows. Aunty nearly had a sinking spell on the front walk. It had taken her many a weary year to come this far.

At the door we handed over our invitation to a hired man of some sort. Then right away a lady in gray lace and gussets with a single long strand of pearls was making for us. "Mrs. Fleischacker, how good of you to come. It is only a family party with a few friends." She seized Aunty's hand, which must have been like ice. "I thought it was time we met," the lady said.

This was Mrs. Danforth Evans herself. Behind her in a long room couples swept past in the waltz to the strains of "Every Leaf on the Tree." Granddad was remarkably subdued, but it wouldn't last. Buster looked wary, though when Mrs. Evans shook his hand, he said, "At your service, ma'am."

Mrs. Evans called us all by name. She lingered over Lottie, but who wouldn't? She was that pretty. Then we were led into a library shelved to the ceiling. Before a veined-marble fireplace stood a very sleek man with wings of gray hair and gold-wire spectacles. He was Mr. Evans, though his wife referred to him as the dean. He came forth and lingered over Lottie's hand too.

Granddad stirred and came alive. "Si Fuller," he boomed, "from down in Christian County." The rug on the floor was an Aubosson, as Aunty later recalled. Granddad looked around, possibly for a spittoon.

"Mr. Fuller, I am given to understand that you are a well-known figure in your district," Dean Evans said in greeting.

"Well, I'm an old sod-bustin' son of the soil, and an early settler in them parts. I'm older than I show," Granddad imparted. "I got more toes than teeth."

"You don't say so," the dean replied smoothly. "Are you a drinking man?"

"Only on special occasions," Granddad said, "and this is one of them."

A young man turned up suddenly in the library door. He ran his hand through his hair, looking rushed. He was broad-shouldered and right good-looking, all in black with a boiled shirtfront and patent-leather shoes. "Mother," he said to Mrs. Evans, "why didn't somebody tell me they were . . ."

Then he saw Lottie. She stood by the hearth, all in lavender that brought out her eyes. Her hands were clasped before her to keep them steady.

"Lottie?" the young man said. "Lottie."

"Everett," Lottie answered.

"Hecka-tee," said Granddad.

Come to find out, Everett wasn't a drifter and a grifter after all. And he'd never done time in jail. He'd been in college. He was pale and spindly from his studies at the University of Chicago. That summer he'd come down to work in the field for our neighbors the Shattucks to build himself up. There he'd caught his first sight of Lottie.

Despite her feelings Lottie hadn't encouraged him overmuch. She hadn't turned him away either, though she saw the differences between them. Him trying to educate her by reading to her from his schoolbooks hadn't worked on his behalf. As she was to say, she hadn't minded the poetry, but she didn't care for the history. It was all about the past, and she was looking ahead. Still, it was a warm summer, and Lottie melted.

And wasn't she sly? She let Mama send her up to Chicago to get her away from Everett. And right along she knew he'd be coming home to get ready for his senior year. Let this be a lesson to all mothers everywhere.

The members of my sex can be very sly. Give me boys every time. One of them asked me to dance that night at the Evanses. I told him I didn't know how, not unless it was a square dance. But the orchestra wasn't playing "Turkey in the Straw." It was playing "After the Ball," the song the whole world sang that summer. But the boy swept me up anyway, and while I didn't float, I didn't fall.

Lottie and Everett turned past us on the ballroom floor, and they only had eyes for each other. In a far corner Granddad seemed to be lecturing several professors from the university. Over there along the paneled wall Aunt Euterpe had found her place in the society of refined ladies looking on as chaperones from a row of gilt chairs. Where Buster was, I couldn't tell you. He was quicksilver, there and gone before you knew.

We saved the great wheel on the Midway for our last evening. It was the famous invention of the bridge builder George W. Ferris, meant to be an answer to the Eiffel Tower at the exposition in Paris, France.

We stood long in the line to get on, and Everett Evans was with us. He and Lottie were too thick to stir now, and a little sickening in the looks that passed between them.

There we stood with that great metal thing creaking and groaning over our heads. I believe that was the last time in our lives that Buster clung to my hand. And Aunt Euterpe wasn't looking forward to getting on it either now that she seemed to have something to live for.

But at last we were at the head of the line and being hurried into one of the cars. They held sixty people, and forty could sit on upholstered swivel chairs.

Then up we began to go, leaving our stomachs behind. Up as high as the minarets of A Street in Cairo, then higher than that until you couldn't even hear the music from the Midway. I thought about not looking. Aunt Euterpe sat stuck to her chair, clutching her reticule in a death grip. Everett and Lottie gazed only upon each other. But Buster and Granddad were plastered to a window, so I looked too.

As we turned up into the sky, you didn't notice the straining and the clanking of that terrible wheel anymore. The great exposition began to fan out below us, and all the pavilions were like frosted wedding cakes. It was the White City on blue lagoons against the endless lake. Golden statues caught the last of the setting sun. Then like sudden morning the electric lights came on. If

I could show you anything, I would show you that. The searchlight turned, and everything was washed in light like there could never be darkness again.

Just at that moment when the fair was a field of diamonds beneath my feet, the fair and all the world belonged to me. Rosie Beckett of Christian County.

Granddad's weathered old cheeks were wet with the beauty of it all, and Buster's eyes were saucers. There was the future unfurling below us as we rose higher and higher into the bright night.

After the Ball

L ottie and Everett were married in the library of the
Danforth Evans residence in the summer after the
fair. Of course we were all there. Dad gave Lottie away.
Buster was her ring bearer, which he didn't like being. I
was her maid of honor. While I leaned to pink, she had
me in powder blue, with a wreath of cornflowers to quiet
my red hair.

I sang at her wedding, the first time I'd sung without
her voice to carry me since that distant day when they'd
had to lead me off the stage. I sang "O Perfect Love," and
Mama's hand reached over to take Aunt Euterpe's. Mama
had a hat for the occasion, with lilacs.

Lottie and Everett urged me to live with them in

Chicago and go to high school there, and Mama and Dad let me do it. Though I thought I had about all the education I could absorb, the fair convinced me I had a world more to learn.

Aunt Euterpe pursued her plan to sell her house on Schiller Street and move into a hotel. She chose the Metropole on South Michigan Avenue. There she was welcomed into the society of that neighborhood as kin of the Danforth Evanses.

Dad had been right as rain when he said he'd never make a farmer out of Buster. Buster wasn't more than nineteen before he was in the east, in the state of New Jersey, looking for work in the motion pictures.

He mastered the Kinedrome, the machine that made *The Great Train Robbery* starring Bronco Billy Anderson. Later on Buster followed the movies to California, where the world came to know him as LeRoy Beckett, the producer of Westerns—first one-reelers, then two.

And Granddad? He never died. He lived on and on, in our hearts. I see him yet, stumping along the Midway in his old ice-cream traveling togs, parting the common people with his stick.

Or there he goes in his terrible wreck of a buggy, the buzzard's feather in his hatband to ward off rheumatism and the epizootic. Tip's there on the seat beside him, and they're going to town for the mail, in case one of us children has written a letter home. And, of course, it's always fair weather.

After the Fair

A Note from the Author

The World's Columbian Exposition closed forever on October 30, 1893. Monday, October 9, the twenty-second anniversary of the great fire, was named "Chicago Day," and 754,261 visitors passed through the fair's turnstiles. Chicagoans called this the largest gathering of humanity in the history of the planet. The New York newspapers, still aggrieved that the grandest of all fairs had been held a thousand miles from civilization on the verge of empty prairie, once more skewered Chicago for its boasting as the "Windy City."

On October 28 Mrs. Potter Palmer presided over the ceremonial last meeting of the Board of Lady Managers, ascending the platform in the Woman's Building to the

VIEW FROM THE SEARCHLIGHT (CHICAGO HISTORICAL SOCIETY)

boom of an organ prelude, Miss Susan B. Anthony at her side.

Across the fairgrounds in the Hall of Music, the Honorable Carter Henry Harrison began to ring down the curtain on the fair before a convention of his fellow mayors. "This World's Fair has been the greatest educator of the nineteenth century . . . It has been the greatest educator the world has ever known," he said. "I myself have taken a new lease of life, and I believe I shall see the day when Chicago will be the biggest city in America."

The White City on the shores of the inland sea reached for the sky and promised a steam-driven, electrically lit future of peace and prosperity through progress.

But the fair ended on an ominous note.

When Mayor Harrison returned home from his last speech, he was shot dead at his front door by an assassin. The final night of the fair had been planned as a spectacular sound and light show, but in mourning for the mayor, the flags were lowered in silence, and all "music, oratory, and pyrotechnical displays" were canceled. The fair closed with the tolling of a funeral bell, and the huge Westinghouse searchlight made a final sweep of the grounds and went dark.

Still, the World's Columbian Exposition altered the future and changed the face of the nation in large ways and small. The ideal vision of a city rising out of pools and plazas informed city planning through the century to come. The fair's Greek and Roman pavilions reappeared in many a pillared and porticoed public building. The exotic Japanese and Turkish architecture inspired the revolutionary designs of a young Chicago architect named Frank Lloyd Wright.

The fair inspired another Chicago man, L. Frank Baum, to create a mythical land in his series of books beginning with *The Wonderful Wizard of Oz*. The White City became, on the page, the Emerald City. The Czech composer Antonín Dvořák was moved by the fair to write his *New World Symphony*, and Scott Joplin went on to syncopate a new century in ragtime.

The fair's founders aimed to educate the populace, but the populace flocked to the fair, and the Midway, to have a good time. They rode George Ferris's great wheel for the thrill and the view, not because it was a mechanical miracle. The wheel that had become the true symbol, the Eiffel Tower, of the fair outlived it to be set up again in St. Louis for the Louisiana Purchase Exposition of 1904. Only then was it dismembered, and its metal bones now lie under the Forest Park golf course in St. Louis.

But not before it inspired thousands more, smaller Ferris wheels. The Midway itself, with its bouncy blend of beer gardens, bears on bicycles, peep shows, joy rides,

BUFFALO BILL CODY (CHICAGO HISTORICAL SOCIETY)

and such personalities as Lillian Russell, Gentleman Jim Corbett, and the gyrating Little Egypt became the American carnival, touring every small town by rail and road before it took root again and became the theme park. Buffalo Bill's Wild West and Congress of Rough Riders of the World outgrossed both fair and Midway, inspiring a new, purely American entertainment, the rodeo.

The world was never the same again. Products introduced in the pavilions and along the Midway—hamburgers, carbonated drinks, Cream of Wheat, Juicy Fruit gum among them—became staples of the consumerist society.

Perhaps a more important legacy of the fair was the collective memory of those who glimpsed its wonders as their first vision of the world as it was, and as it might be. In millions of minds the great wheel kept turning in the summer sky above the incandescent White City that seemed to banish darkness and doubt.

PHOTO CREDITS

ABOUT THE AUTHOR

Richard Peck, the acclaimed author of more than twenty-five novels, has received numerous awards for his work, including the Newbery Medal for *A Year Down Yonder,* the Newbery Honor for its prequel, *A Long Way from Chicago,* and the Margaret A. Edwards Award for lifetime achievement in young adult literature. Mr. Peck grew up in Decatur, Illinois, and now lives in New York City.